DANA 11/12   W9-BQT-237

END ZONE

END ZONE

Tiki Barber and Ronde Barber
with Paul Mantell

A Paula Wiseman Book
Simon & Schuster Books for Young Readers
New York London Toronto Sydney New Delhi

For AJ, Chason, Riley, and Ella
—T. B.

For my three roses
—R. B.

SIMON & SCHUSTER BOOKS FOR YOUNG READERS
An imprint of Simon & Schuster Children's Publishing Division
1230 Avenue of the Americas, New York, New York 10020

SIMON & SCHUSTER BOOKS FOR YOUNG READERS is a trademark of Simon & Schuster, Inc.
For information about special discounts for bulk purchases,
please contact Simon & Schuster Special Sales at 1-866-506-1949
or business@simonandschuster.com.
The Simon & Schuster Speakers Bureau can bring authors to your live event.
For more information or to book an event,
contact the Simon & Schuster Speakers Bureau at 1-866-248-3049
or visit our website at www.simonspeakers.com.
Book design by Krista Vossen
The text for this book is set in Melior.
Manufactured in the United States of America • 0712 FFG
Library of Congress Cataloging-in-Publication Data
Barber, Tiki, 1975–
End zone / Tiki Barber and Ronde Barber ; with Paul Mantell.
p. cm.
"A Paula Wiseman book."
Summary: Co-captains Tiki and Ronde Barber lead their junior high teammates to the Virginia state football championship.
ISBN 978-1-4169-9097-0 (hardcover : alk. paper)
ISBN 978-1-4424-5240-4 (eBook)
1. Barber, Tiki, 1975—Childhood and youth—Juvenile fiction. 2. Barber, Ronde, 1975—Childhood and youth—Juvenile fiction. [1. Barber, Tiki, 1975——Childhood and youth—Fiction. 2. Barber, Ronde, 1975——Childhood and youth—Fiction. 3. Football—Fiction. 4. Twins—Fiction. 5. Brothers—Fiction. 6. African Americans—Fiction. 7. Conduct of life—Fiction.] I. Barber, Ronde, 1975– II. Mantell, Paul. III. Title.
PZ7.B23328En 2012
[Fic]—dc23
2012006268

ACKNOWLEDGMENTS
The authors and publisher gratefully thank Mark
Lepselter for his help in making this book.

EAGLES' ROSTER
9TH GRADE HIDDEN VALLEY JUNIOR HIGH SCHOOL

HEAD COACH—*SAM WHEELER*
DEFENSIVE COACH—*PETE PELLUGI*
OFFENSIVE COACH—*STEVE ONTKOS*

QB
MANNY ALVARO, GRADE 8
HAYDEN BROOK, GRADE 8

RB
TIKI BARBER, GRADE 9
LUKE FRAZIER, GRADE 8

TE
JONAH JAMES, GRADE 7

OL
PACO RIVERA, (C), GRADE 9

DL
ROB FIORILLA, GRADE 7
DANNY HALPIN, GRADE 8

LB
HENRY WELTMAN, GRADE 8

WR
FRANK AMADOU, GRADE 7
FELIX AMADOU, GRADE 7

CB
RONDE BARBER, GRADE 9
JUSTIN LANDZBERG, GRADE 8

S
ALISTER EDWARDS, GRADE 8

K
ADAM COSTA, GRADE 9

SPECIAL TEAMS
RIO IKEDA, GRADE 7

CONFERENCE SCHEDULE
PREVIOUS GAMES AND RESULTS

EAST SIDE MOUNTAINEERS (H): W, 35–17
NORTH SIDE ROCKETS (A): W, 42–35
BLUE RIDGE BEARS (A): W, 29–28
PULASKI WILDCATS (A): W, 26–24
JEFFERSON PANTHERS (H): W, 54–14
MARTINSVILLE COLTS (H): W, 35–17
WILLIAM BYRD BADGERS (A): W, 49–3
PATRICK HENRY PATRIOTS (H): W, 57–20
MARTINSVILLE COLTS (A): W, 38–3
NORTH SIDE ROCKETS (H): W, 42–17

UPCOMING GAMES

BLUE RIDGE BEARS
PULASKI WILDCATS

CHAPTER ONE

A BUMP ON THE HEAD

TIKI BARBER DIDN'T LIKE IT—NOT ONE BIT.
He was sitting at his usual spot, on the bench in the locker room. Surrounding him were his Hidden Valley Eagles teammates, all of them hooting and hollering, psyching themselves up for the game against the Blue Ridge Bears.

The game hadn't started yet. It wouldn't start for another ten minutes, in fact. Yet the Eagles were acting as if they'd already won!

Tiki glanced over at his identical twin, Ronde. The Eagles' star cornerback returned his sober look. They were the only two players who weren't acting like fools.

"I'm gettin' two TDs today," crowed Felix Amadou, the Eagles' star wide receiver. "Oh, yeah!"

"I'm gettin' three! Count 'em, fool," his identical twin brother, Frank, shot back. It was weird, thought Tiki, that the Eagles had two sets of identical twins on the roster.

Tiki and Ronde had purposely tried out for different positions—Tiki on offense, Ronde on defense. But both

1

Amadou twins were wide receivers. That meant they had to share playing time—unless the Eagles were in spread formation. When the Amadous were *both* out on the field, with Tiki at halfback, quarterback Manny Alvaro was armed to the teeth with great offensive weapons.

"Fifty points today," Manny offered up. "Tiki, what do you say? How many TDs we gonna score?"

"I say we ought to quit talking so much."

"Gee," Manny said, taken aback. "What's up with you, man?"

"Nothing," Tiki insisted. "It's just . . . aw, never mind."

A few of the others shook their heads in confusion. "Whatever," Manny said. "Long as you're sure you're okay."

"I'm fine, okay?" The rest of the Eagles left him alone after that. They kept on joking about what a breeze today's game was going to be. The Blue Ridge Bears hadn't been a good team for ten years, and this season, they were even worse than usual.

The Hidden Valley Eagles, on the other hand, were undefeated, and in sole possession of first place. They had been crushing their opponents for the past six weeks, and hadn't had a really close game since week four against their archrivals, the Pulaski Wildcats.

But Tiki had a long memory. He and Ronde had been through a lot during their three seasons with the Eagles. They'd even won the state championship last year. And one thing Tiki had learned was that *nothing worth having ever came easy.*

The past six weeks had been *way too* easy. The Eagles were too comfortable, too confident. To Tiki, his team-mates looked ready for the picking. And had they already forgotten the final score of their last game against the Bears, way back in week three? The Eagles had come away with a big, fat, *one-point* victory!

He wanted to say something, but he didn't want to be a killjoy. His buddies had every right to be confident—and negative thoughts were the last thing they needed before a game.

The trouble was, Tiki couldn't shake those negative thoughts out of his own head. Looking over at Ronde, he knew his twin was thinking the same thing. It happened all the time—a look they shared that meant they both knew.

The look they were sharing now.

The game started well enough. Ronde received the open-ing kick and returned it to the Bear's twenty-five. But that's when it all began to fall apart.

The Blue Ridge defense pulled an all-out blitz on third down. Manny never saw them coming. Just as he was rearing back to throw, he got creamed from behind.

Tiki tried his best to block the outside linebacker, but it didn't matter. Manny had already coughed up the ball.

Even worse, the Bears safety had recovered it and was running it back the other way for a touchdown!

"Aw, man!" Tiki yanked off his helmet and had to stop himself from throwing it down on the ground. That might make him feel better, but it also might draw a stupid penalty for unsportsmanlike conduct.

This was just what he'd been afraid of. All that overconfidence was gone now. He knew going in that the Eagles would be fine as long as things went well—but how would they react now, when they were staring at a seven-point gap?

Ronde took the kickoff, but his blockers were overwhelmed before he could even get a runback started. The Eagle offense had to start operations deep in their own territory.

Now it was up to Tiki. He told himself to hang on to the ball, keep his head down, and run straight ahead every time. The Eagles needed him to steady their offense, and he proceeded to do just that.

Five straight times, Manny handed him the ball, and Tiki pushed the defense back for a grand total of seventeen yards.

Finally, they had enough breathing room for Manny to go to the air. But on his first passing attempt, Felix Amadou caught his spikes on the grass and fell, just as the ball was coming his way! The cornerback was right there to grab it, and the next thing anyone knew, the Bears were driving again.

Blue Ridge had played the Eagles before, and their quarterback knew enough not to throw in Ronde's direction. They had no such respect for the Eagles' other cornerback, Justin Landzberg. Justin was victimized twice—once on a double move by the receiver, and once when the tight end blocked him out on a cross pattern. A leap into the end zone, and one extra point later it was 14–0, Blue Ridge.

Sure, it was early, Tiki reflected. Plenty of time for the Eagles to come back. But their bubble of invincibility had been pierced. The Bears had to be feeling that they could actually win this game. And that made them very dangerous. Sure enough, Blue Ridge continued to play inspired ball, dominating time of possession.

The Eagle offense had gone nowhere the entire first half, when, with just over a minute left, Tiki sank to one knee in the huddle and told himself, "I've got to take over this game. Now." He shot a look at Manny, and the quarterback called Tiki's number.

Tiki took the handoff and started toward the line—then did a sudden reverse and sped toward the far sideline. All day long he'd been attacking the middle, and now he'd caught the Bears by surprise. By the time they recovered and started to give chase, he'd already notched a big gain. Then he dragged two defenders ten more yards, all the way down the Bear thirty!

"Time-out!" Coach Wheeler yelled from the sideline. Everyone trotted over to him, including Tiki, who was still catching his breath. "Okay, Eagles, let's poke it into the end zone right here. They're looking for Tiki, and they're gonna get him—but not in the way they think. Let's try the direct-snap play."

A whoop went up from the excited Eagle offense. They'd never tried the direct-snap play except in practice. It was a trick play, to be pulled out of the bag only in an emergency.

Well, this was an emergency for sure, Tiki thought as he lined up to the right of Manny, just a little closer than usual. Paco Rivera snapped the ball, and Manny pretended to grab it—but instead, it went directly to Tiki. He dashed three steps to his right, and found Felix Amadou streaking for the end zone.

Tiki let the ball fly. It wasn't a perfect spiral. Tiki hadn't done that much throwing in the past, except back when he was a little kid. But he put enough into the throw so that only Felix could reach it.

Felix's fingertips brushed the ball, but it bounced upward as he fell. From the end zone turf, he reached back up and grabbed the floating ball before it hit the ground. Touchdown, Eagles!

Adam Costa added a quick extra point, and the final seconds of the half flew by. When the Eagles got to the locker room for their fifteen-minute break, they were more relieved than confident. But soon enough, the over-confidence started making a reappearance.

"They got so lucky that half," Justin Landzberg said. "They're not getting another one by me today."

"And Felix falling down?" Manny put in. "When does that ever happen, yo?"

Tiki was fuming. He'd known this would happen! It was like he could see it coming. Yet he'd chosen not to say anything before the game. What was the matter with him?

Hadn't he learned anything these past three years? Hadn't he watched his mother speak out and stop a factory from polluting their neighborhood? Hadn't he seen how well his big speech to the whole school went over, once he found the courage to say it out loud, in front of everyone?

These were his best friends. His teammates. Why was he so afraid to get up and speak his mind, to them of all people?

This was the time. This was his last chance to say something. He told himself to get up and take the floor. He and Ronde were co-captains of the team now, after all. They had a right to address the team whenever they wanted to.

Tiki looked at Ronde. Ronde stared right back at him. Tiki understood that they each wanted the other to speak first.

The seconds went by. People started conversations with one another. Kids cleaned their cleats or adjusted

7

their padding. Some went to use the restroom.

Maybe he didn't need to say anything, Tiki thought, looking away from Ronde. After all, they were only seven points down now . . . and if he spoke to the team too often, they might stop paying attention. He thought of the story of the boy who cried wolf so often that, when a real wolf appeared, no one listened to his warnings and the wolf ate all their food.

The band came off the field, their halftime performance done. They crowded past the team in the locker room, on their way to the music room where they would store their instruments.

Halftime was over. It was time to strap their helmets back on and take the field again. "Why didn't you say anything?" Ronde muttered to him as they headed for the field.

"Why didn't *you*?" Tiki shot back. It wasn't really an answer, but then, Ronde didn't have one either. The moment had passed, and neither team captain had seized it. Tiki only hoped it didn't cost them later on.

The opening kickoff was a disaster. Just like in the first half, the Bears caught the Eagles flat-footed. The returner was small and had good moves. The Eagles were flying at him, but they were missing sure tackles!

Before they knew it, the little guy was in the end zone, spiking the ball and doing a war dance. He got penalized for clowning around too much, but who could blame him for celebrating? He and his team were on the verge of handing the mighty Eagles their first defeat of the season!

Ronde took the kick, and got fifteen yards out of the runback, which was the best he'd done since the opening kickoff.

Manny handed off to Tiki a couple of times, but the Bears were waiting for him, and the gains were small. Third down and nine, and Coach called a pass play, naturally.

The only problem was, the Bears knew it was coming, and they sent everyone straight at the quarterback. Manny got the pass off, but Tiki and Luke Frazier, the fullback, weren't able to stop the third blitzer. Manny got hit, and his head slammed right into the turf.

The Bears trotted back to their huddle, but Manny remained on the ground. Tiki ran over and knelt by his side. Soon they were surrounded by worried Eagles, including Coach Wheeler, the offensive coach, and the team trainer.

The trainer helped Manny up into a sitting position and stared hard into his eyes. "You okay, son?" he asked.

"I'm fine," Manny said, but he sure didn't look it. His eyes were crossing and uncrossing, and he looked like he was going to do a flop any second.

"Bring a stretcher," the trainer called. "Just a precaution, son," he told Manny. "You're gonna be fine. We're just gonna have you checked out for a concussion, okay?"

"No!" Manny protested, trying to stand up but having to lean on Tiki for support. "I can play. Coach, tell him I can play," he begged Wheeler.

"Kid, your health is more important than this game, or even this whole season," Wheeler said firmly. "Don't worry, Hayden will get us through till you get back out here."

"I'll be back for the next drive," Manny said as the stretcher arrived and they loaded him onto it. "Just keep it on the ground till then. I'll get us back in this game."

"Sure thing," Wheeler told him, but Tiki could tell he was lying. Wheeler stared after Manny as the stretcher was taken off the field.

The fans applauded, but they sure looked worried. And Tiki knew it wasn't just Manny they were worried about. Without their regular quarterback, could the Eagles come back from fourteen points down?

"Maybe he'll be back," Paco said hopefully.

"Don't count on it," Wheeler said. "If he's got a concussion, and it sure looks like he has, he won't be back for a while. Certainly not for this game."

"But Coach—!" Paco and some others started to protest.

"Don't 'but Coach' me," Wheeler told them sternly. "Manny's health comes first. We'll just have to find a way to win behind Hayden."

Tiki blew out a breath as Hayden Brook, a seventh grader who had a lot of talent but who had hardly played all season, came trotting out onto the field. Tiki saw his eyes before he pulled his helmet on. Hayden had the look of a deer in the headlights.

"Don't sweat it, kid," Tiki told him, trying to sound sincere. "You're gonna be great. Just hand me the ball, and let's get back into this game."

Tiki turned to the rest of the guys in the huddle. "Listen up," he said. "Where's all that confidence I was hearing in the locker room? Is this a one-man team?"

"No," most of the kids said, but not really loud.

"That's right! Every one of you is better than the guy he's facing on the other side of that line. If each of us does his job, we'll win this game!"

"Yeah!" they said, a little louder this time.

"Now, come on! You just beat your man, one play at a time!"

"Yeah!" It was a real shout this time. They clapped in unison, and broke the huddle.

From that moment on, the Eagles mounted a long, grinding comeback. Tiki ran the ball more times than he ever had in a single game. He only got three, four yards most carries, but somehow, he kept their drive going all the way to the end zone.

After the extra point, it was 21–14, Blue Ridge. Only seven points to make up!

That seemed to inspire the Eagle defense. They rose

up to stop the Bear attack, and handed the ball right back to the offense.

Hayden kept on giving Tiki the ball, and Tiki kept on running like a man possessed. He logged fifty-nine yards on the drive! Hayden ended up throwing only once, and it took Blue Ridge by surprise. Even Jonah James seemed surprised as he caught the ball for the touchdown.

After the game-tying extra point, it fell to Ronde to save the game for Hidden Valley. So many times over the past two and a half seasons, he'd pulled the Eagles' bacon out of the fire. Game after game, he'd stretched his small frame to the limit, intercepting or knocking away a pass, saving a sure touchdown.

Now that he'd finally hit his growth spurt and caught up to Tiki's size, his stride was longer, he could leap higher, and his longer arms could reach balls that used to elude him.

Now, in the game's final minutes, when he saw the Bear quarterback about to throw to the other side of the field, Ronde made a quick decision. He left his man uncovered. Suddenly acting like a free safety, Ronde closed the distance in a heartbeat, and leaped high into the air to intercept the pass!

"Wow!" Tiki yelled from the sideline, leaping along with his twin. "He came out of nowhere! Did you see that?"

With time winding down, the Eagles got the ball at

midfield. He was nearly exhausted, but there was no stopping Tiki. He pounded much bigger defenders, knocking them flat on their rear ends as he bulled ahead for yardage like a fullback.

Finally, on the Bear three-yard line, with first and goal, a surprise play came in from Coach Wheeler. "Quarterback reverse!" Hayden told them.

Another trick play! Hayden took the snap, faked a handoff to Tiki, then turned and ran toward the sideline, as if he were out of the play . . .

. . . except that he had the ball tucked behind his back! When Hayden snuck into the end zone, it sealed the Eagle victory at 28–21, and saved them from a terrible loss that would have tarnished their perfect season.

Tiki was so happy, so relieved, and so exhausted, that only after he'd showered and changed did he realize he'd forgotten something very important.

He found Manny in the trainer's room. "Hey, dude," he said, "how's your head?"

Manny frowned. "I told Coach I could go back in there, but he wasn't having any. So go ask *him* how I am."

Tiki could see Manny was upset. He felt like saying, *It's okay, man—we won the game. We're still undefeated!*

But he knew Manny would take it the wrong way. When people are angry, Tiki knew, sometimes it's best not to try to reason with them.

"The main thing is, you're okay," he finally said, clapping Manny on the back and retreating.

"I'm fine, man," Manny insisted. "Totally fine. It was just a little bump on the head. No big deal."

Tiki nodded. He sure hoped Manny was right.

CHAPTER TWO

SUPERSTITION

RONDE WAS FEELING GOOD. THE TEAM HAD HAD a scare, for sure—but the only thing that mattered was the final score. He couldn't help smiling as he looked around at the rest of the Eagles. They were close—almost like a family. They'd been through something amazing together—and they'd just had a big reminder of how incredible it was to be where they were.

"Do you know the last time there was an undefeated team in this league?" Coach Wheeler asked as they gathered around him.

None of them did.

"1965."

A few low whistles sounded in their midst. "The last undefeated team that also won the *League Championship* was in 1954."

"Wow," Ronde said, along with several others.

"I want you to look around this room," Wheeler said. "Look into the eyes of these young men who are your teammates—the ones you rely on week in and week out."

Ronde caught Tiki's eye and they both smiled. Coach Wheeler had come a long way from the beginning of last year—his first game as a coach. They'd *all* come a long way. And there was nobody better than Coach Wheeler to remind them that they were on the brink of something very special.

"You guys are one victory away from an undefeated season. You are three victories away from being undefeated League Champs! I'm sure there have been undefeated *State* Champs—I didn't look that one up—but if we get that far, just imagine . . . Take a moment and picture yourselves there. . . ."

The room grew silent. "Okay," Coach finally said. "Now I want you to *forget* all that, and concentrate on only one thing—next week's game against Pulaski. I don't have to tell you about them. Last time, we beat them by one point—and they're a whole lot better than the Blue Ridge Bears. Nobody's going to hand us this prize. We're going to have to get it on our own.

"So from this moment on, it's one game at a time. It's one *play* at a time. Each of you will have to reach deep down inside himself, if we're going to achieve our goals. Remember character is everything in the game.

"Now go home, but don't lose your focus over the holiday weekend, because you'll be mentally ready when game time comes. Of course, that doesn't mean you can't enjoy yourselves—eat some turkey, have some laughs, and remember how lucky we all are to know one another. Be thankful that we're Eagles!"

There was a thunderous cheer, and people began pounding on their lockers to make even more noise. Ronde was really enjoying it—but then he saw Manny covering his ears and wincing in pain.

"Hey, guys, that's enough!" Ronde shouted, motioning for calm. "Let's go—everyone's waiting for us outside."

They filed out of the room—all except for Tiki, Manny, Coach Wheeler, and Ronde.

"You okay, Manny?" Ronde asked.

Manny sprang to his feet and headed for the door. "I'M FINE!" he yelled. "When is everybody going to stop asking me that?"

The door slammed behind him, leaving Tiki, Ronde, and Coach Wheeler to look at one another in bewilderment.

"Ma, this is the best turkey ever!" Ronde said. But with his mouth stuffed full, it came out more like "Mafishbshtrkvr!"

"Ronde Barber!" their mom scolded him. "How many times have I told you boys—"

"Not to talk with our mouths full!" Tiki finished for her. But of course, it sounded more like "Mtkfmfsfl!"

Mrs. Barber had to laugh, even though she did set high store by good manners. Ronde knew she took great pride in her cooking, and turkey dinner wasn't something the family had every day, or even every month.

"Mind your manners, both of you!" she scolded, trying hard to frown. "Now, before we move on to the desserts—"

"Desserts!" cooed Aunt Flora, her eyes widening and her hands coming together as if in prayer. To Aunt Flora, who was more than slightly chubby, dessert was something to be prayed for—and nobody's desserts were better than Mrs. Barber's.

"Why, Geraldine, you are something else! How do you do it all?"

Mrs. Barber beamed. "The *boys* made the dessert," she declared.

Aunt Flora's smile weakened just a bit. "Oh?"

"Yes! It's Jell-O and marshmallow pie."

"Jell-O and . . ."

"Marshmallow. Lime Jell-O. With whipped cream."

"Oh!" Aunt Flora said. "I'm sure it's delicious—but I am rather stuffed."

"Flora, no!" Mrs. Barber said. "I won't allow you to refuse. The boys are famous for their Jell-O-mello pie. Aren't you, boys?"

"We sure are!" Ronde and Tiki said, slapping five across the table.

"Mmm. Well, then," said Aunt Flora, giving them each a smile. "I suppose I must try just a little. . . ."

"As I was saying," Mrs. Barber resumed, "before we have dessert, I would like us all to say what we're most thankful for this year."

Ronde saw Tiki roll his eyes. He knew how his twin felt. Sometimes, their mom could seem corny. But that was only if you weren't paying close attention. Really, she was trying hard to teach them the right way to live, so they'd grow up to be good, successful men. And being thankful for what you had was a big part of that.

"I'll start," said their mom. "I'm thankful for the jobs I have—the jobs that put this food on our table. Lord knows it was hard to get them, and it's hard to keep them too. I'm most thankful for my two wonderful sons, and for our family. . . ." Here, she looked at Aunt Flora, Uncle Henry, and their three children, Kwame, Patrice, and Theo. "All right, who's next?"

Everyone said what they were thankful for. Tiki talked about being a star on the Eagles, how he was thankful for getting good grades and having the world's best mother . . . and brother. "I'm thankful for *all* the gifts I've been given—and the mind to use them well," he finished.

"Very good, Tiki!" Aunt Flora said. "My, doesn't he speak well."

Then it was Ronde's turn. He was shyer than Tiki, and Aunt Flora's words made him not want to say anything at all. But he didn't want to be embarrassed, so he found his courage, and began.

"I'm thankful for Mom, and for Tiki, and that I finally got bigger." Everyone laughed. For about six months, while Tiki shot up more than an inch a month, Ronde hadn't grown at all. Finally, he'd caught up, and the twins were the same size again at last.

"I'm also thankful for the gift of being good at sports . . . at football in particular. I don't like to say it, because I don't want to jinx it, but, well, we're close to having an undefeated season, and—"

"SHHH!!" Tiki said. "Don't talk about that! It's bad luck."

"Nonsense," Mrs. Barber said. "It's how you play on the field, not what you say off of it, that makes you win or lose."

"Oh, I don't know," said Aunt Flora, with a worried look on her face. "A black cat crossed my path last month, and the next day, I broke my wrist!" She held up her left hand, which was still wrapped in a sling.

"Nonsense," Mrs. Barber repeated under her breath. "Oh, well, I think it's time for dessert. Tiki and Ronde, would you like to do the honors?"

Both boys didn't wait to be asked twice. They sprang up and rushed toward the kitchen, colliding twice in the narrow hallway that connected the dining room to it.

"Get out of my way!" Tiki said, pawing his way ahead of Ronde.

"*I'm* getting it!" Ronde shot back, yanking on Tiki's shirt.

They both grabbed the tray at the same time, from either end.

"Okay, we've both got it," Ronde said.

"Give it over," said Tiki, tugging on it lightly.

"You!"

"No, you!"

"Boys?" came their mother's voice from the dining room.

Seeing that Tiki was momentarily distracted, Ronde grabbed the tray out of his hands and rushed for the dining room.

"Hey!" Tiki yelled, and leaped after Ronde. His toe caught Ronde's heel in the middle of the narrow hallway, and the tray went flying. First it hit the big mirror in the hallway, cracking it in two places. Then the Jell-O-mello pie fell right on Tiki and Ronde's heads.

Everyone laughed when they saw the boys with the Jell-O and marshmallows on them. Everyone except their mother, who had her hands to her face and was staring at the hallway.

"My good mirror!" she gasped.

Aunt Flora gasped too, and rose from her chair with a shocked look on her face. "Oh, no!" she cried. *"Seven years bad luck!"*

"She's full of baloney," Tiki said. "Seven years bad luck, my foot!"

He lay in bed, staring at the ceiling. Ronde lay in his own bed, across the room. The company was just saying good-bye downstairs, but the two boys had long since been banished to their room for the night.

"What if she's right?" Ronde said in a loud whisper. "What if—?"

"Just be quiet," Tiki told him. "If you hadn't been so selfish—"

"Me? If you hadn't lunged at me—"

"If you hadn't—"

"Never mind!" Ronde said. "Forget it. You're probably right. It's just a silly superstition."

"Exactly."

The room fell silent, and soon, Ronde could hear Tiki snoring softly. He wished he could sleep too. Then he wouldn't have to keep thinking about all the disasters that might happen if Aunt Flora just happened to be right.

It was a long holiday weekend. Friday lazed by and faded into Saturday, with its college football games on TV, and Sunday, with the NFL broadcasts. Of course, it wasn't all sitting on the couch and staring at the screen. The cousins stayed right on into Saturday afternoon, so there were street football games too.

Tiki and Ronde had fun, but they didn't play full-out. Their cousins were younger, and not as athletic, and besides, neither twin wanted to take the slightest risk of injuring himself. They had broken that mirror, after all—and who knew whether the old superstition had some truth in it?

But by Monday morning, they'd forgotten all about it. There had been no other mishaps. Ronde was starting to think he'd been a fool to give that broken mirror more than a moment's thought—other than he and Tiki having to pay for it out of their savings.

Morning classes went quickly, and a pop quiz in math kept him focused on his schoolwork all the way till lunch period.

This was what he'd been waiting for. The chance to hang out with the rest of the Eagles at their unofficial table, to talk football, and Pulaski, and maybe going undefeated for the regular season—something even last year's State Champion Eagles hadn't done.

The gang was there, all right—all the usual suspects. More than half the team took lunch this period, and most of them chose to eat together. Usually, it was a pretty raucous corner of the cafeteria—but not today. Everywhere Ronde looked, there were glum faces staring back at him, or down at the table, or just into space.

"What's up?" Ronde asked. "It looks like a funeral around here."

"Manny's out," Paco said. "Have a seat and join the pity party."

"Huh?"

"He's out, Ronde," Adam said. "As in, he's not playing this week."

23

"Next week, either, probably," Justin added.

"What the—?"

"Concussion, dude," Paco explained. "He was having headaches after the game, so they took him to the doctor, and he's got to shut it down."

"For how long?" Ronde asked, sinking down into a chair. Suddenly, he felt sick to his stomach. The smell of food in the cafeteria, which had been making him hungry up till that moment, now had the opposite effect.

"Whenever they give him the 'all-clear' to play. Could be a week, could be a month." Paco sighed. "What are we gonna do now?"

Ronde shook his head. He had no answers.

None of them did.

CHAPTER THREE

THE MIRROR CRACKED

TIKI BOUNCED INTO THE CAFETERIA, FEELING ON top of the world. In his hand was his latest English composition, with a big red A+ marked on top of it. "Yeah, baby, that's what I'm talkin' about!" he said, showing it off to some kids he knew at the nearest table.

He remembered way back in seventh grade, when he'd first arrived at Hidden Valley Junior High. He recalled how shy he'd been, afraid to raise his hand or speak up in class. That all seemed so long ago now. He'd given a speech in front of the whole school that had gotten a standing ovation. They'd even asked him to write an advice column in the school paper because they thought he was so together. And of course, everyone knew and loved him as the co-captain of the Eagles.

He was sorry this was his last year here. In September, he'd be a lowly freshman at Hidden Valley High School. No more being top man on the totem pole. Probably riding the bench on the football team too, like he had back in seventh grade.

Maybe not, though. Coach Spangler at the high school

knew Tiki and Ronde. He'd seen some of their games. Tiki hoped he'd put them right into the starting lineup, so they could team up with their friend Matt Clayton, who was the star quarterback there.

Still, it would mean starting from scratch. Here, he'd built up so much on the way to this moment. He was one of the most popular kids in school—and if the Eagles went undefeated and won the State Championship again, he'd go out a legend, never to be forgotten at Hidden Valley Junior High. . . .

Those were his thoughts as he approached the Eagles' unofficial tables. But when he saw them all, with their long faces and their hurt puppy-dog eyes, every happy thought went right out of Tiki's head.

"Okay . . . what?" he asked, sitting down in a hurry.

When they told him the bad news about Manny, Tiki had to fight back the sudden urge to hurl. He wanted to run away as fast as he could, to a place where none of this had happened, where the team's future still looked bright, shiny, and perfect.

"What are we going to do?" he asked, more to himself than to anyone else. No one answered him, anyway.

Tiki couldn't manage to eat his lunch that day. Neither, he noticed, could Ronde. Most of the other players hadn't done too well on their food either.

Manny Alvaro was only an eighth grader, of course. Not a star like Matt Clayton used to be at quarterback, or even a standout passer like Cody Hansen last year.

Still, your quarterback was your quarterback. Manny was a great scrambler. That helped his receivers get free. Manny and Tiki had always had a great rhythm together too—rarely did a handoff or a quick pass get dropped.

Hayden, by contrast, was a big, tall kid who could throw the ball a mile—but he had zero game experience. And this one against Pulaski was the biggest game of the season—against the Eagles' most dangerous opponent! How could they expect Hayden to step into Manny's shoes and guide them to victory?

The Eagles all parted ways to go to their classes. Tiki felt alone, almost in a bubble, as he walked down the hall. He ignored all the hands raised in attempted high fives. The calls of "Yo, Tiki!" sounded like they were coming from miles away. GO, EAGLES! posters covered the walls in every hallway.

The image of the broken mirror came into his head. All those pieces of shattered glass on the floor . . .

"Wait a minute!" he told himself, stopping dead.

"Oof!" Someone bumped into him from behind. "Hey, what are you—oh, Tiki! Sorry, man, didn't know it was you." The kid clapped him on the back and kept going, while Tiki stared ahead, lost in his own thoughts.

"I can't let some stupid superstition beat me," he told himself. "I'm *Tiki Barber*, and Barbers know how to *play proud*."

He began walking again, this time with a sense of purpose, as if he was on a mission. "The team can't count on Hayden to lead us. So the offense is gonna have to lean on me."

He knew he could handle the weight. He'd done it before, whenever the team was down for the count, and looking to him to come through. There was no reason he couldn't do it again—one more time, or two more times, or even three if he had to.

"Tiki?" his math teacher, Ms. Brownstein, wore a puzzled look as she watched Tiki walk right by her door. "Aren't you coming in?"

Tiki turned around and came back, feeling a little embarrassed. "Sorry," he told her. "I was thinking about something else."

"Well, think about it later," Ms. Brownstein told him. "We've got work to do on our theorems."

Tiki tried to concentrate, but it was hard. His thoughts kept coming back around to the gigantic task ahead of him. Sure, he always wanted to be THE MAN, but now he *had* to be. That was different.

Sure enough, when he got to practice that afternoon, Coach Wheeler took him into his office. "Sit down," he told Tiki. "We have to talk."

Tiki sat and waited for Coach to talk.

Wheeler flipped through his playbook, then closed it and looked straight at Tiki. "Against Pulaski's defense, we've always featured a passing game, because of all those massive guys they've got on their D-line. But not this time, Barber. This time, we're gonna have to go to *you,* early and often. You know why?"

Tiki nodded. "Yes, Coach."

"Right. Hayden's got a great arm, but he's all over the place. And his nerves are gonna be jumping from the get-go." He paused, and looked right through Tiki. "You got beat up pretty bad last game yourself. How you holding up?"

Tiki shrugged. "I'm fine. Totally. No problem." He'd been sore right through the weekend, but he didn't tell Coach that. No reason to. He felt okay now, that was the important thing—and his team needed him. Enough said.

"Okay, then, Barber. We're gonna run every play in this book that features you. We're gonna run you like we've never run you before—and after that, we're gonna run you some more. When you've got nothing left, we'll go to Luke."

Luke Frazier was the fullback, and also served as Tiki's backup when he needed a breather.

Tiki grinned. "I got this one, Coach," he said. "Count on it."

"Good. Let's go out there and practice." They shook hands as they got up. "This is history we're talking about here, remember."

"Oh, I know that," Tiki said. "Believe me, I never forget it."

· · ·

They went through their paces at half-speed. Coach didn't want to wear Tiki out—the game was only three days away, and nearly every play they practiced featured him.

Everyone knew (but didn't say) the obvious: If anything happened to Tiki—if he got hurt or sick—the team at this point, without Manny, had no plan B. Pulaski would not be forgiving. The Eagles had only one route to victory on Thursday, and Tiki was it.

They worked in a couple new plays too—new blocking schemes, and a reverse handoff from Tiki to Hayden off a direct snap. This was a variation on something they'd done with Tiki and Manny. But Hayden had never practiced it, and since he was a lefty, Tiki had to line up on his other side.

They gave Jonah James, the tight end, new responsibilities, having him be an extra blocker for Tiki on some of the outside runs. Five thirty came before they knew it, and it was time to call it a day and go home.

Tiki was leaving the locker room when he ran into Cootie Harris, the team mascot. "Hey, Cootie!" Tiki greeted him. "What are you doing here so late?"

Cootie looked both ways before whispering, "I'm in glee club."

"Oh. That's cool."

"You mean, you're not mad?"

"Mad? Why should I be mad?"

"Oh, just 'cause I'm supposed to be working hard as team mascot, not pursuing other interests."

"That's wack," Tiki told him. "I was writing a column for the school paper, remember? Answering letters from readers like you."

"I remember," Cootie said. "Thanks for the help, by the way."

"You already thanked me."

"Right. Point is, you quit, because it was distracting you from your main thing."

"Right. But . . ."

Cootie looked at him. "But what?"

"Nothing," Tiki said. He'd been about to say that while Tiki was actually playing in the games, Cootie was just leading the cheers. But then he realized, just in time, that Cootie was probably as passionate about what he did as Tiki was about his own "main thing." So he said nothing. Instead, he clapped Cootie on the back and said, "You ready for Thursday?"

"*So* ready," Cootie said, beaming. "Perfect season, here we come! Hey, with you and Ronde, how can we lose, right?"

"Uh . . . right," Tiki said, trying to sound more confident than he felt. He sure hoped Ronde and the defense would do their part, holding the vaunted Pulaski offense to a couple touchdowns at most.

"Oh, by the way," Cootie said. "Don't tell anyone, but I've got a bet going with Fisher Smith, the mascot for Pulaski."

"A bet?"

"Yeah! Whoever's team loses, that mascot has to go to the other school and parade around their cafeteria, *in costume*." He giggled at the thought of it. "He's gonna be so humiliated!"

"Uh, yeah," Tiki said, feeling even more antsy.

Cootie suddenly seemed to realize that there was another possibility. He turned to Tiki, his eyes wide. "Oh, no. Promise me you won't let that happen, Tiki!"

"I . . . I promise," Tiki said, regretting the words already. Sure, it was bad luck to say things like that—a jinx, they called it—but what choice did he have? What else could he have said to Cootie? He *had* to promise—to guarantee victory!

Great, he thought, as he went outside to meet Ronde for their ride home on the late bus.

As if he didn't have enough pressure on his shoulders already!

CHAPTER FOUR

BAPTISM BY FIRE

THE MOMENT TIKI GOT ON THE BUS, RONDE KNEW something was up with him. On the silent ride home, he tried to imagine what his twin was going through. It wasn't that hard to figure.

Sure, it would be tough—for all the Eagles—to make up for Manny's absence. But at least the defense would be playing at full strength. Ronde's job would be the same as always.

For the offense, it was a different story. All the blockers would have to work doubly hard—and, in addition to their regular plays, they would have to remember all the new ones put in for Tiki and Hayden.

Those two were under the most pressure of anyone, Ronde knew. Hayden, because he—who had rarely even gotten to play, and never when it really counted—was suddenly stepping into Manny's key role.

But on the field, Ronde reasoned, things would actually be tougher for Tiki.

No one was expecting much from Hayden Brook. And he wouldn't be called upon to pass very much, unless the Eagles fell far behind.

As for Tiki, not only would he be expected to do his usual magic—this time, he'd have to be the Eagles' "Mr. Everything."

No wonder Tiki didn't feel like talking, Ronde thought. He tried to keep the conversation light over the mac and cheese dinner their mom had left for them before going off to her second job, where she had to work until ten o'clock.

Only late that night, as they lay in their beds in the dark, did Ronde speak up, in a soft but firm voice. All evening, he'd been thinking of what to say and how to say it, and he figured it was now or never.

"Tiki?"

"Huh?"

"Listen, I've just gotta say something."

"So, who's stopping you?"

"Right. Well, I just want to say that you've been under pressure before, and most times you've come through just fine. Flying colors, man."

"I know," Tiki said. "But this is different. We've got a perfect season on the line, and it all comes down to me."

"Not *all*," Ronde corrected him. "The whole team has to come through. Not just you. If the blockers don't do their job, you can't do yours. If the defense doesn't get us the ball back, you won't have time to do your thing. It's a team game, Tiki, no matter how much we all depend on you."

"I keep thinking of Manny," Tiki confessed. "We've got to win this one for him."

"We've got to win it for *all of us*," Ronde said.

"Why does it have to be Pulaski?" Tiki moaned. "Why couldn't it have been some easy team like Jefferson or Martinsville?"

"There are no easy games," Ronde said. "Not when you have this much on the line. Might as well climb the highest mountain, not the lowest."

They fell silent again, and Ronde racked his brain for something else to say. At last, he fell back on humor. "Hey, if you get too tired, we can switch uniforms at halftime, and I'll go out and be you."

That got the desired result—a stifled hoot of laughter from Tiki's side of the room.

"Seriously!" Ronde said in mock anger. "What's so funny? I know all the plays from practicing with you in the street!"

"Those Wildcat receivers will have you too tired out to play offense," Tiki said.

"What? Give me a break! I'm shutting them down, brother. They are not scoring. Not one time."

"Just concentrate on your own thing," Tiki told him. "I've got my end."

"You sure now?"

There was a second's silence. Then, "I *said* I've *got* it."

"All right, then," Ronde said. "G'night."

"Night."

Ronde hoped that he'd helped lift some of the cloud

that was following Tiki around. But hope was all he could do. He fell quickly to sleep and dreamed of disaster on the field.

The bad luck started early, with the Wildcats winning the toss and electing to receive. On the opening kick-off to Pulaski, Ronde was shoved from behind, knocking him out of the play just as he was about to tackle the ball-carrier.

He came up yelling for a penalty, but the refs had missed the foul, and he knew it wouldn't help to argue. So Pulaski started its first drive deep in Eagle territory.

Ronde and company kept them from scoring that first time, but the Pulaski punt landed Hidden Valley on their own thirteen yard line.

Tiki started off on fire, bursting through the line for eight yards, then another six, then another seven. But soon Pulaski wised up, and started shifting extra men onto "Tiki-watch."

The Eagle drive began to sputter, bogging down at their own thirty when Tiki kept getting dragged down for no gain. Adam had to punt, and once again, the Wildcats began a drive in good field position at their own forty-eight.

This tug-of-war went on for the whole first quarter of the game. But each time the Eagles got the ball, they were farther back in their own end. And each time Pulaski took over, it was deeper into Eagle territory. Finally, early in the second quarter, they pushed it across the goal line for the game's first touchdown.

The Hidden Valley crowd had come primed for a perfect end to their perfect season. Instead, the game had started out in the worst possible way.

Pulaski had been a juggernaut all season. Except for their one-point loss to the Eagles in week three, the Wildcats hadn't lost a single game. If they beat the Eagles this time, by more than one point, *they* would be crowned league champions instead of Hidden Valley!

Cootie looked miserable, even though he had a big phony smile plastered on his face. "Gimme an *E*!!" he yelled through his megaphone, and the crowd responded. "Gimme an *A*!!"

But there was a note of desperation in his voice. Nobody wanted the Eagles to have to come from behind—not against a team like Pulaski.

Ronde gave the Eagles hope with a great runback to the Eagle forty-three. Then Tiki managed to rip himself free of three Pulaski defenders, and break down the sideline all the way to the Wildcat sixteen!

But that was as far as they got. Pulaski's defense was big and fast, and they knew who was getting the ball every time—Tiki. They piled on him like concrete blocks, and every time he got up from the bottom of the pyramid, he looked more tired and sore than the time before.

The Eagles managed an incredibly long field goal, thanks to good old Adam Costa, who basically never missed. *Well,* thought Ronde, *at least we're on the scoreboard.*

Ahead by 7–3, Pulaski went to work on their next drive, striking through the air. They completed short passes to their tight end, their halfback, and even their fullback, taking them all the way to the Eagle thirty. So far, they'd avoided Ronde completely, and had even avoided Justin at the other corner, by throwing short up the middle, forcing the Eagle linebackers into coverage.

Ronde knew that couldn't last. Sooner or later the Eagles would overreact and cover too tightly. That's when the Wildcats would throw the bomb.

Sure enough, after two running plays were stuffed by Rob Fiorilla, the Eagles' big defensive end, the Wildcats went to the air, this time for all the marbles.

Naturally, they threw to Justin's man. Ronde had built up a reputation over three years at Hidden Valley as a shut down cornerback. Most teams tried to stay away from him. But not many teams had two great receivers to throw to. Pulaski did.

The ball beat Justin by a fingernail, settling perfectly into the receiver's hands for a brilliant TD. An extra point later, and it was 14–3, Wildcats. Cootie looked like a drowning man as he kept trying to rally the forlorn Eagle fans.

Ronde shot a glance over at Tiki. His twin looked worried but determined. Ronde decided that Tiki still had his mojo working, so he didn't say anything to him. Instead, he jogged onto the field and got down to business, returning the kickoff forty yards to the Wildcat thirty-nine. "There you go, bro," he told Tiki as they crossed paths—Ronde on his way off the field, Tiki heading back on.

"Way to play, Ronde!" Tiki told him. "Watch me now."

"Walk the walk, brother!"

Tiki was relentless. He'd run the ball every play but three this half. Anyone would have thought he'd be exhausted by now. But here he was dragging two defenders all the way down to the twenty yard line!

Two plays later, the Eagles were at the fourteen, but it was third down now, with four still to go. Tiki was bending over, sucking air into his lungs. Coach Wheeler beckoned him over to the sideline and sent Luke Frazier in with the play.

Ronde patted his twin on the back. "Great job," he said.

"I couldn't . . . go . . . any more. . . ." Tiki said between big breaths.

"No sweat," Ronde told him. "Luke is going to—"

No sooner had he spoken than he wished he'd kept his mouth shut. Luke got slammed backward for a two-yard loss. Now it was fourth and six from the sixteen, and Adam had to salvage something from the drive by nailing another field goal to keep the Eagles within eight points.

"Twenty seconds left in the half," Ronde muttered, strapping on his helmet. "I'm gonna get us a touchdown right now."

He didn't care if it was bad luck to talk about things you were going to do before you did them. Right this minute, he just wanted to focus like a laser beam, radiate confidence, and force himself to do his very best.

The ball came to him, end over end, but he made sure he had it firmly in his grip before he got started. He put a dazzling juke move on the first defender to reach him, then sidestepped another before darting forward, splitting two more Wildcats and getting into the open field!

The crowd roared, urging Ronde on. He reached midfield, the forty, the thirty, the twenty—and was tripped up at the sixteen yard line!

"Dang!" he said, smacking the ball before handing it back to the ref. "I almost had that one!"

There were still six seconds left in the half. "Go get 'om, Tiki!" Rondo shouted as they crossed paths again.

"One time!" Tiki shot back, giving Ronde a thumbs-up. "Nice going, bro!"

Ronde could only watch now. One play—six yards—seven or even eight points. It could happen . . . it *had* to happen . . . !

The ball came to Tiki—surprise, surprise—and the Wildcats were on him in an instant. One of them punched at the ball, trying to knock it loose. But somehow, Tiki held on to it—and broke free of his defenders! He was down to the two . . . and now three more Wildcats piled onto him!

He wrestled with them, refusing to go down . . . and reaching out with the ball, he stretched out, trying to put it over the goal line. . . .

SLAM!

A hand reached out and smacked the ball free! It rolled around in the end zone. Ronde jumped up and down as first one Eagle, then another, leaped for the ball only to have it squirt away.

Finally, it was picked up by one of the Pulaski safeties, who ran it out of the end zone and was suddenly out in the open field, heading for the *other* end zone!

"NOOO!!!!" Ronde moaned, along with two thousand fans in the bleachers, as the kid reached paydirt and spiked the ball in triumph.

Ronde sank to his knees and looked back at the near end of the field. There was a yellow flag on the ground! Ronde got up, jumping up and down and awaiting the referee's call.

"Holding—Wildcats!" he shouted. "After the fumble, Wildcat ball at their own six yard line, first down!"

The disappointed Wildcats lined up opposite the relieved Eagles, and the quarterback took a knee to end the first half. The Eagles trotted off the field, still in the game, but facing a 14–6 score that looked like a very high mountain to climb.

In the locker room, Ronde sought out his brother. He knew Tiki must be near his wit's end. What could he say to inspire him, to get him ready to play the best second half of his life?

He sat down and put an arm around his brother's shoulders. "You did great."

"Yeah, great," Tiki said sarcastically. "I could have had that touchdown, but I let the ball get knocked away—like an idiot."

"Hey! That was a good play. There was nothing else you could have done there."

"I could have gone down at the two, with the ball in my hands."

"But time would've run out!" Ronde pointed out. "You *had* to reach out with it."

Tiki looked up at him. Ronde saw that his eyes were filling with tears. Tiki fought them back, gritting his jaw. "They're all over me, Ronde," he said.

Then, to Ronde's surprise, Tiki grinned. "Sure you don't want to switch with me for the second half?"

"Ha!" Ronde laughed. "That's rich, dude. Like I could really do that."

"You could," Tiki said. "You said so yourself."

"I was just flossin'. You know I wasn't serious."

"I know. Still, right now, it's a tempting offer."

"Hey—just get back out there and play your game."

"I've *been* playing my game—what more can I do?"

Ronde sighed. "Look, I know *you're* tired, but man, you're tiring *them* out too! I saw them all sucking wind, just like you. It's just a matter of who's in better shape to play the next thirty minutes."

Tiki snorted. "Nobody's in better shape than us," he said.

"That's right!"

"They really were sucking wind?"

"Would I lie? Don't answer that question."

Now it was Tiki's turn to laugh—and Ronde saw that he had succeeded in breaking the spell. His brother seemed lighter now, ready to get back out there and grind it out.

"Listen," Ronde told him, "just forget all that garbage going through your head, okay? Remember what you said on Thanksgiving."

"What was that?"

"Don't tell me you forgot already! You said you were thankful for all your gifts and for the mind to use them well."

"I said that?"

"That's right."

"That's pretty good."

"You got that right. Now get out there and use that mind. Maybe get a little creative, and show 'em a few surprises."

"Surprises?"

"You know what? Hayden can run. Maybe you might want to look for him when they're all over you."

"A little lateral action?" Tiki looked intrigued.

"Just a thought," Ronde said, grinning. "Hey, life's full of surprises—why not show Pulaski a few?"

"Not bad," Tiki had to admit. "I'll run it by Coach and Hayden."

"Make sure you give credit where credit is due, now."

"Ha! I am just full of brilliant ideas," Tiki teased.

"Take credit for it if you want; what do I care? Just go out there and love the game."

"You're full of good stuff today, Ronde. You know, you ought to write an advice column."

"Oh, no, don't get started now." Ronde laughed.

"Seriously, thanks. You're the best, brother."

"Best one you ever had, huh?"

"Hey—let's go play proud." Tiki put out his hand.

"Play proud, yo," Ronde agreed, giving Tiki their secret handshake—the one they'd used since way back in pee wee league. "Let's go win us a football game."

CHAPTER FIVE

CRUNCH TIME

TIKI SQUEEZED HIS BROTHER HARD. HE KNEW HE was lucky to have Ronde. In spite of their occasional arguments, they were as close as two brothers could be. Closer even than that, because they were identical twins.

It was really something special to have someone out there in the world who was so much like you that they thought the same thoughts at least half the time.

Tiki meant it when he'd said his piece at Thanksgiving dinner, about how grateful he was for his brother. And his mom, too. He knew he had a lot to be thankful for—but if he didn't get out there and somehow change the course of this game, the biggest prize of his life would escape his grasp.

Oh, sure, Hidden Valley was going to make the play-offs anyway. They'd probably wind up playing this same team again in the play-offs. But there was something about a perfect season that was different.

Last year had been special because of all the Eagles had overcome—they'd only narrowly escaped elimination several times.

But this year was just the opposite. *Everyone* expected them to win. If they didn't, the whole school would be devastated.

"Okay, Eagles, let's get out there and take back this game!"

Tiki blinked. The coach had been talking for a while, but Tiki'd been so involved in his own thoughts, he'd missed the whole speech!

Coach Wheeler's voice was hoarse, as it usually was this time of the season. The team cheered and lined up to run back onto the field. Tiki and Ronde waited till the last, exchanging their secret handshake one more time.

The second half did not start well. Ronde ran the kickoff back for forty big yards—only to have the whole thing called back by a penalty! Rio Ikeda, one of the Eagles' young stars on special teams, had allowed himself to get too pumped up, and he'd blocked one of the Wildcat rushers in the back.

Rio came off the field looking forlorn. "Hey, chin up, dude!" Tiki told him. "We need you to be your best this half—no moping around. We're gonna win this game, and you're gonna be a big part of it!"

Rio smiled and nodded. "Thanks, Cap'n," he said.

Tiki didn't have to look down at the *C* stitched onto his jersey to feel it burning into his chest. It was all about playing proud. That was the message their mom had taught him and Ronde, and that was the message they, as

Eagle co-captains, tried to pass along to their teammates every day.

Coach Wheeler called in the play: Texas Tech. It was a sweep, with everybody blocking for Tiki. Up till now, the game plan was to have Tiki charge straight into the line. with off-tackle plays down after down. They hadn't gained much yardage, but at least they'd tired out the Pulaski D-line.

Hopefully, they wouldn't have the wind left to chase Tiki all the way across the field and tackle him before he could turn the corner.

The ball was snapped. Hayden slammed the ball into Tiki's chest. Tiki grabbed it and ran for all he was worth, straight along the ten yard line. He turned the corner, shook off the fingertip tackle attempt by the Wildcat defensive end, and turned it up into the backfield.

Twelve yards later, the safety slammed him out of bounds. But Tiki could see that Coach's strategy was going to work. If they hadn't caught him this time, no way would they catch him later in the game, when they were *really* tired.

If the Eagle defense could stuff the Pulaski attack, he and the offense would make sure the team came all the way back.

After a quick pass to Jonah James, it was Tiki time again. This time, the sweep went left instead of right, because the ball was spotted on the right hash marks, which gave the Eagles more room to their left.

It worked again, netting eight yards, and keeping the drive going. But once they were in the red zone, the defense stiffened up. With less room to maneuver, and the backs closer to the line of scrimmage, it was harder to gain ground. In the end, they had to try another field goal. Even worse, this one was blocked!

Now Tiki could only watch, and hope that the Eagle defense was up to the challenge of keeping the game close. On first down, Pulaski tried a sweep of their own—but Ronde sniffed it out, running all the way across the field to make the tackle and hold the Wildcats to a short gain.

On second down, they tried a quarterback draw. This time, it was Rob Fiorilla who made the great play, grabbing the quarterback's sleeve as he went by and dragging him off-stride, so that the rest of the defenders could throw him for a loss.

It was third and ten, and everyone, including Tiki, knew that, in spite of the fact that they were deep in their own end, the Wildcats would have to pass. Tiki watched, his eyes fixed on Ronde as his twin kept stride for stride with Pulaski's number one receiver.

Coach Pellugi had sent out an extra defensive back so that they could double-team Justin's man. That left Ronde in single coverage. It was bait, and Pulaski's quarterback went for it, throwing a long bomb to his number one guy.

The ball was thrown well, and the receiver was taller

than Ronde—even though Ronde was a lot bigger than he used to be. But Ronde made up for it with tremendous speed and leaping ability—not to mention great hands. Without breaking stride, he took to the air and grabbed the ball away from the receiver!

Ronde fell to the ground, but the ball stayed firmly in his grasp.

"Attaboy, Ronde!" Tiki threw a fist high into the air as he ran back onto the field.

Hidden Valley started from their own seventeen yard line. But with Tiki running side to side, and Pulaski running out of energy, the Eagles were suddenly unstoppable. The only time they didn't make major gains was when Tiki had to go to the sideline for a quick breather.

Ten plays later, after a slow but powerful drive, he leaped over the pile of linemen and into the end zone! It was now a two-point game, and Coach called for a two-point conversion attempt to try and tie the game.

Tiki felt sure Wheeler would call his number, but instead, he called for a fake handoff and quarterback roll-out to the weak side. Tiki would surely have complained if he'd been on the sideline, but in the huddle, there was no one to argue with.

Besides, he knew what Coach was thinking: Pulaski would be putting everyone on Tiki-watch. It only made sense to surprise them.

It would have worked, too, if Hayden hadn't tripped

over his blocker's foot and tumbled to the ground. A moan went up from the home crowd when they realized their heroes were still behind in the game, 14–12.

Pulaski's offense stayed on the ground, keeping away from Ronde at all costs. They wound up having to punt, but not before moving the ball into Eagle territory.

On the Eagles' next drive, Tiki found he was getting tired again. He was a step too slow on the sweeps, twice in a row. Then he saw Coach Ontkos waving him off the field!

"What's the deal?" he asked after he made it to the sideline.

"I'm giving you a rest till the fourth quarter," said Coach. "Let Luke tire them out for a while. Then we'll get you back in there when we've got better field position."

"I'm not tired, Coach!" Tiki protested—but he knew he was.

"Tiki, it's important to be patient. Remember, it's the score at the end of the fourth quarter that counts."

With Luke running on fresh legs, the Eagles managed to push the ball nearly to midfield. But a lot of time was getting run off the clock, and because Coach didn't trust Hayden to pass more than once in a blue moon, they had to stay on the ground and use up precious time.

The fourth quarter started with a punt to Pulaski that was run back all the way to midfield. Tiki cringed. Hidden Valley couldn't afford to fall any further behind— not when they had no passing game!

The Wildcats wasted no time on their attack, going to the air on first down and coming up with fifteen yards by throwing at Justin's man. Then they tried pounding it forward on the ground, but Rob Fiorilla, who was having the game of his life, stuffed them twice in a row.

That's when something happened that blew Tiki's mind. Pulaski's quarterback dropped back to pass, and was looking for his tight end, when Ronde appeared to stumble, allowing his man to get two steps on him!

"Oh, no!" Tiki moaned, and he wasn't the only one who noticed. The quarterback quickly turned and fired, going for Ronde's man as he streaked toward the end zone.

But amazingly, Ronde got there first! From the moment the quarterback released the ball, Ronde turned it up into another gear—a gear even Tiki didn't realize he had.

He caught up to his man and outjumped him for the ball, for the second time that half! He came down at the one yard line, but hey—it was Eagles' ball, and they only needed a field goal to take the lead!

"Get back in there, Barber!" Coach said, clapping him on the back. "How you feeling? Still tired?"

"No, Coach!" Tiki shot back, grinning. "I never was tired. I told you that!"

"That's my boy," he said. "Keep those feet moving, now."

Tiki dashed out to the huddle. "Miami, on three," said Hayden—an off-tackle run for Tiki—back to the original plan.

This time, the defense seemed a step slower than before. They had their hands on their hips and were sucking in air after the play, which netted eight yards.

On second down, Tiki blasted through a gigantic hole created by Paco throwing his weight around. When he finally went down, he was at the forty-two yard line!

"Texas Tech on one!" The sweep again. Tiki took the ball and went flying toward the sideline, then turned the corner untouched. When he saw the safety about to knock him out of bounds, he did a quick 360 and turned back toward the hash marks. The safety went flying off the field and right into poor Cootie!

Tiki could hear the crowd roaring in his ears as he crossed midfield and headed into Wildcat territory. When they finally tripped him up, it was at the Pulaski thirty-eight.

Tiki looked up at the clock. Only three minutes left, but they were getting close to Adam's field goal range. All they had to do was keep going. But Tiki needed a breather, and he knew it. Raising his hand, he signaled to be replaced.

With him out of the lineup, the Eagles were unable to advance. So after only one play, Tiki ran right back onto the field, trying to reach deep down for his last reserves of strength.

"Miami on two," said Hayden. Another blast through the line.

"Clear 'em out, Paco," Tiki told him.

"They're already gone," Paco replied. "Consider it taken care of."

Paco was as good as his word. Another gaping hole in the line allowed Tiki to break through and gain nine yards—just enough for an Eagle first down as the two-minute warning sounded.

Tiki needed the breather, but he knew it gave Pulaski a rest too.

"Let me throw one, Coach," Hayden begged. "They'll never expect it—we haven't hardly thrown all game. I know I can hit Frank or Felix in the end zone! Please?"

Coach Wheeler frowned, and so did Tiki. They both knew Hayden was right. But Tiki also knew that Hayden had no game experience passing the ball, and that their whole season was on the line right here. If they didn't score on this drive, they might not get the ball again before time ran out.

"I'm sorry, Hayden," Coach said, as Tiki sighed with relief. "I've got to stick with what got us here. Next year, it'll be a different story."

Hayden kicked the dirt, but he nodded, too, to show that he was on board.

"Hey, kid," Coach Wheeler told him. "Don't get down, now. You've been great out there today. Make sure the handoff goes without a hitch."

Hayden nodded again and managed a sort of smile. He and Tiki ran back out to the huddle together.

Here it goes, Tiki thought. *Everything's on the line right now.* He took the handoff, and when he saw that there was no hole, he waited, looking for an opening. He ducked out of reach of the first man through the pile, then saw what he was looking for!

It was just a sliver of daylight, but it was going to have to be enough. Tiki hit it hard, and so fast that no one had a chance to react. Then he was into the open, heading for paydirt! All he had to do was—

"OOF!"

He was hit so hard that he nearly let go of the ball. But something, some instinct, made him grasp it harder, just as the hands started grabbing for it in midair. He landed with the ball still in his possession, and the Eagles were at the Pulaski thirteen.

There was one minute and thirty seconds left in the game. For most of those incredibly long ninety seconds, Tiki felt like he might not have the strength left.

But there was one thing he'd forgotten to mention during that Thanksgiving dinner speech—something he was everlastingly thankful for now. That was his superb conditioning under Coach Wheeler. He'd built himself up into a powerhouse runner, and now he came to see that his endurance had also grown.

Pulaski was out of gas, but Tiki still had an ounce left in his tank. It took five brutal runs, but that last ounce put him over the goal line. It took the Eagles over the top, all the way to that perfect regular season they'd been dreaming about for months!

The touchdown came with only one second left on the clock, and time ran out during Adam's squib kickoff. The game, and the regular season, was over. The Eagles had done it—and without their regular quarterback!

"Man!" Ronde could not keep the grin off his face. It had been plastered there ever since the final gun sounded. Here it was dinnertime, and he was still flying with joy. "I can't believe we did it!"

Ronde's words brought the wave of happiness back over Tiki, too. He beamed, stuck his tongue out, and shook his head. "I know," he said.

"I'm so happy, I feel like running around the block and screaming my head off."

"Ronde, I can barely move my body, let alone run."

It was true. Tiki had run the ball at least forty, maybe fifty times in the game. He'd taken the worst pounding of his life from those gigantic Pulaski defensemen.

Everything hurt. He was black-and-blue all over his upper arms and thighs. He'd rolled his ankle in the postgame madness, dancing and jumping around the field, hugging players, fans, Coach. . . .

It had been a great day, and it wasn't over yet. Tiki knew where Ronde was coming from. The day didn't feel complete, somehow. Neither twin was ready to let go of it.

"I know!" Ronde suddenly said. *"Manny!"*

"Riiiight," Tiki agreed.

Poor Manny had had to watch the game from the bleachers. Even though he looked and seemed fine, even though he'd been a part of the celebration afterward, his happiness could not have been as complete as theirs. After all, they'd won *in spite* of him, not *because* of him.

"Let's go over to his house and surprise him!" Ronde suggested.

"We could bike over. It's only, what? Eight blocks?"

"Hey, let's bring him a piece of Mom's victory cake!"

Mrs. Barber had missed the big game. It was a first—she almost always came to their games, especially the big ones. But things were very busy at her job, and her boss told her that, if she kept missing time, he'd have to dock her salary.

She was still at work, and it was after eight o'clock. But she'd left the boys their favorite dinner to heat up—her famous mac and cheese—and there was something extra in the fridge, too—a small cake with a football and the word VICTORY etched in the icing.

"Now, how did she know we'd win?" Ronde wondered.

"She didn't," Tiki said, smiling. "She just believed in us, that's all."

They both fell silent, feeling how lucky it was to have someone who believed in you—especially if it was your mom.

"But that would mean . . ."

"That I'd be out for the entire play-offs."

Suddenly, Tiki felt his whole world turn upside down. He and Ronde exchanged alarmed looks. If Manny couldn't play, the Eagles would have to somehow win behind Hayden Brook.

That would mean game after game of Tiki getting pounded. Could he take that kind of punishment and still be a force on the field?

If he couldn't—if the Eagles failed to repeat as State Champs—everyone would say it was his fault!

In an instant, one of the best days of his life had become one of the worst!

"Come on, yo," Tiki said. "Cut Manny a piece and let's go."

Manny was surprised to see them. Tiki could see that he was glad they'd come—but he could also tell that Manny was trying hard to stay upbeat.

"We sure could have used you, dude," Tiki told him. "I hurt all over."

"Sorry," Manny said, his smile fading. "Sorry . . ."

"Hey, now," Tiki said, "I didn't mean it like that."

"No, Manny," Ronde added. "It's not like that—if you'd been playing, the game wouldn't have been close."

"Besides," Tiki said, "now that we're both in the play-offs, we'll probably be playing them again really soon."

"I think we actually get them first," Ronde said.

Manny sighed. "I know. That's the trouble."

"Trouble?" Tiki didn't like the sound of that word.

"What do you mean, trouble?" Ronde said quickly.

Manny swallowed hard. "Well, the good news is, I didn't have any headaches today."

"Great!" Ronde said. "That's fantastic."

"But this is the first day I haven't had any. And the doctor says that even light concussions sometimes need a month or more to heal."

"A—a month?" Tiki stammered.

"Or more?" Ronde moaned.

Manny nodded. "That's what he said."

CHAPTER SIX

BE PREPARED

THE NEWS HIT RONDE LIKE A BRICK. WITH MANNY at the helm, they'd had a good chance of winning the State Championship. In fact, they'd been the favorites, at least according to the *Roanoke Reporter*.

Without Manny, the Eagles had two chances—slim and none.

They'd barely beaten Pulaski today, with Tiki doing double duty! They'd *never* be able to do that again. Tiki was moving now like he was eighty years old. The next game was less than a week away. Hayden Brook was going to have to be the "man"—or at least, the "Manny"—until the real Manny came back. Which might be never, as far as this year was concerned.

Ronde and Tiki put on brave faces, smiled big smiles, and told Manny to hang in there. "You'll probably be back in a couple days," Tiki told him. "You'll see."

Manny shrugged. "The doc said we'd play it week by week. So that means the soonest I can be ready is Wednesday."

"Hey, that's game day!" Ronde said, clapping Manny on the back. "Dude!"

"Yeah, that's *if* he says I'm ready. If not, it's another week of torture."

"Oh, hey!" Ronde said. "We almost forgot. Here, we brought you something." Reaching into his backpack, he pulled out the piece of cake with VICTORY written on it. Except the word VICTORY had gotten all smushed in the backpack. The icing came totally off as he unwrapped it. "Uhh, sorry, dude."

"That's okay," Manny said, taking it from him carefully. "Mmm. Good," he said, tasting the icing with his fingertip.

"It said 'victory'," Tiki told him. "My mom baked it for us."

"Wow. Mmmm."

"Well, enjoy it," Ronde said. "We've gotta get home."

"Okay. Thanks for the cake. And thanks for coming," Manny told them, giving them a sadder but more sincere smile than the one he'd worn when they got there.

Back on their bikes, riding home in the dark, the boys were silent, except for Tiki's occasional grunts when something hurt. Halfway home, he said, "Pull over, Ronde."

They brought their bikes to a halt. "You okay?" Ronde asked.

"Yeah, I'm fine."

"You sure?"

"Yeah, man."

"Then why'd we stop?"

Tiki put a finger to his lips. "Sshhh," he said.

The night was quiet and cloudy. It was cold, too. December was here, and any day now, the first snow of the winter might arrive.

"Look up there," Tiki said, pointing to the top of Mill Mountain. The big neon star glowed brightly in the night, like a beacon in the sky.

There were other stars up there, Ronde knew. Billions of them, hidden by the clouds. But this one, neon, man-made, and five-pointed, seemed to stand for all the others.

"That's our lucky star up there, Ronde," Tiki said softly. "Get a good look at it. We're gonna do this thing. Don't ask me how I know. . . . I just do."

Ronde said nothing. He stared at the star, then at Tiki, whose eyes were glowing with its reflection. Ronde had rarely heard his twin talk like this. In fact, he couldn't think of even one time. He wanted to ask Tiki how he knew, but Tiki had just told him not to.

Ronde was left to wonder whether Tiki even believed what he was saying. He sure seemed to—but maybe he was just trying to convince himself.

But hey, so what? Wasn't that exactly what Ronde had done when he'd talked to Tiki at halftime? Had he really believed half the things he'd said?

Well . . . he *had* at the moment he *said* them, at least. Now, looking back on it, it was hard to tell. Ronde decided to go with the flow; to go with the notion that Tiki had

had a vision—a vision that, somehow, they would make come true.

Suddenly, the chill of the air hit him, and he shivered. "Let's get on home, Tiki," he said. "I'm about to freeze to death."

"Sure thing," Tiki said. He gave the star one last look, then pointed his bike toward home. He was about to shove off, when he turned back to Ronde again. "Hey," he said. "Give me the shake."

Ronde walked his bike next to Tiki's and offered his hand up.

"We're gonna make this happen," Tiki said. "I swear it."

Ronde hesitated for only a second before saying, "Me too."

The brothers exchanged the handshake they'd invented back in peewee league, where this whole incredible journey had started. It was December now. Pretty soon, their football careers at Hidden Valley Junior High would be history.

Would it be a story of triumph? Or would it end in bitter defeat, after this final turn of bad luck?

The image of the shattered mirror rose to Ronde's mind, but he shut it out, forcing himself to keep looking at the Mill Mountain star as they rode home in the dark.

"Atta baby, Hayden!" Coach Ontkos yelled as the QB launched a long pass that landed softly in Felix's arms.

"Look at that. He didn't even have to break stride!"

Hayden smiled shyly, happy to be praised, but not used to all the attention.

He'd better get used to it in a hurry, Ronde thought. *He's gonna get all he can handle.*

Coach Ontkos was responsible for the Eagle offense, and at today's practice, he was devoting most of his time to his new quarterback.

Hayden was looking more confident already. All he needed was experience, Ronde thought, and he'd be a star in his own right. He had a great arm, he threw a ball that was easy to catch, and he was pretty accurate, too—so long as he wasn't being pressured.

That was the thing, Ronde knew. No amount of practice could prepare Hayden for the speedy, huge Pulaski defenders who would be gunning for him. Sure, Hayden had faced the same defense last week, but since the coaches didn't let him pass much, there was never any pressure coming at him.

This week, Coach Wheeler had decided they would show Pulaski a different game plan. Ronde knew this was smart—Pulaski would put extra people on Tiki, and devise new ways to stop the run. If the Eagles wanted to win two in a row from their archrivals, it would have to be through the air.

It was going well today, at any rate. Everyone on the offense was impressed with Hayden's skills and growing confidence in the pocket. When they were done, the sweat streaming down their faces in spite of the sub-freezing temperature, Coach Ontkos gathered them around him.

"Guys," he said, "I'm telling you right now—by game time, you are going to be ready. What we did today was execute our offense in its simplest form. We're gonna keep it simple, because we have to. But that's gonna be enough—trust me—because every one of you is going to execute those few, simple plays to perfection. Understood?"

The boys all nodded, and a lot of them said, "Yeah, Coach!"

Ronde kept silent. He wanted to agree, but inside, he just wasn't sure this was going to work. He had an uneasy feeling he couldn't shake.

It was one thing to execute against your own defense, which wasn't really coming at you hard, trying to knock you flat on your back.

It was a totally different animal to do it in a play-off game, against an opponent as hungry as you. No—*hungrier*. Both teams were shooting for a championship, but the Pulaski Wildcats were also looking for *revenge*.

CHAPTER SEVEN

REMATCH!

THE ARTICLE IN THE ROANOKE REPORTER *CAME* out the morning of the Pulaski game. Tiki and Ronde had known the game would be featured in the sports section. Everybody had been talking about it ever since last week's cliffhanger between the same two teams.

When the paperboy's bicycle bell sounded, Ronde was in the bathroom brushing his teeth. Tiki ran out to grab the paper and get the first look at the article.

By the time Ronde came downstairs, Tiki was at the table, finishing the last paragraph. "Listen to this," he fumed. "'One of Pulaski's star players—'"

"Wait, wait!" Ronde interrupted. "Read it from the beginning. I want to hear every word."

Tiki's jaw tightened. "All right," he said. "It starts, 'Today is the first round of Roanoke's junior-high football play-offs. In the first game, the North Side Rockets will face—'"

"No, man, get to the part about our game!" Ronde broke in.

"I thought you wanted to hear every word."

"About *our* game, not the other one!"

"Okay, okay," said Tiki. "Let's see . . . ah, here it is. 'In the other matchup, the Pulaski Wildcats are looking to get even with their nemesis, the Hidden Valley Eagles. Last week, these same two teams battled to a near-stand-off. But in the end, the Eagles triumphed, behind their unstoppable star running back, Tiki Barber.'"

Tiki stopped reading. He hadn't wanted to read that part at all—it was embarrassing to be singled out like that. Besides, he wasn't really "unstoppable." And saying he *was* put even more pressure on him.

Ronde frowned. "Do they say anything about *me*?"

Tiki bit his lip. "Uh, let's see now . . . yeah, here it is: 'Tiki's identical twin, Ronde Barber, had a key interception in the game. . . .'"

Ronde smiled. "That's better. Keep reading."

"'For the past ten years, Pulaski has been a league powerhouse. Over the past two years, though—in fact, since the Barber twins joined the Eagles—Pulaski has been bested by their archrivals. Already this season, Hidden Valley has beaten the Wildcats twice.'

"'But this time, Pulaski vows the outcome will be different. The whole team seems to be bent on evening the score. "We're going to win this game," said quarterback Jeremy Halper. "I guarantee it.'

"'Linebacker Jeff Tambor was more specific. "We're going to stonewall the Barber brothers," he promised. "If we stop them, the Eagles have no chance."'"

Tiki looked up. Steam seemed to be coming from Ronde's ears, and his eyes were burning with fury. "I'd like to stuff that paper right into their big fat mouths," he muttered.

"Never mind that, Ronde. Take it out on the field, man." Tiki thought for a moment, then added, "You know what I'm going to do?" He folded the paper up and stuck it into his book bag. "I'm going to pin this article up on the bulletin board in the locker room. Just in case any of the guys haven't seen it."

Ronde smiled and nodded. "Good idea. If that doesn't get the team fired up, nothing will."

"*WHAAAT*?" Paco stood staring at the bulletin board, his beefy hands on his even beefier hips. "I can't believe this! Hey, you guys—check this out!"

The team gathered around the article. Tiki and Ronde stood watching them, letting it all sink in, smiling with satisfaction.

"I'm gonna flatten Jeremy Halper," Rob Fiorilla said.

"You're not getting by me today, Tambor," Paco said, sticking his finger at the newspaper. "You're gonna eat your words, you punk."

"Hey!" Tiki said, stepping forward. "Listen up, you guys."

"Listen to what?" Luke Frazier asked. "We already got the message, Tiki."

"That's right," Tiki agreed. "Hey, I'm the one who pinned it up there. I wanted to make sure you all saw it."

The team members murmured angrily. "We saw it, all right," one of them said.

"They're going to be gunning for me," Tiki said, "and they're going to try to take Ronde out of the game too. So it's all on you guys to step up your game. We're counting on the rest of you to rise up and show those loudmouth Wildcats that we're a team, not just a pair of twins surrounded by a bunch of empty uniforms! Are you up for it?"

"YEAAH!!" came the deafening response.

Tiki turned to Coach Wheeler, who had just entered the locker room. "All yours, Coach," he said, giving up the floor to the astonished Wheeler.

As he listened to the coach give his last-minute instructions, Tiki felt a dark shadow come over him. The rest of the team was ready—no doubt about that. Any fear they had felt before was now overwhelmed by their anger at the Wildcats.

But in spite of Tiki's rousing speech, he himself wasn't really convinced. If the Wildcats succeeded in taking him and Ronde out of the game, how would the Eagles—already missing their regular quarterback—find a way to win?

Who would carry the brunt of the offense? Luke Frazier? Luke was a powerful runner, but he lacked Tiki's speed

and moves. Hayden Brook had looked great in practice, but Pulaski's defense would hurl everything in the book at him, once they realized he was actually going to throw the ball this time around.

If the Eagles couldn't score very much, that meant their defense would have to pitch a shutout, or pretty nearly. Would they be able to stop the Pulaski juggernaut, if the Wildcats avoided Ronde like the plague?

The Eagles ran onto the field screaming at the top of their lungs, waving their arms to whip up the crowd noise, which was already deafening.

The Wildcats were already on their sideline, watching calmly with their hands on their hips. They didn't look scared; not the least bit. They looked determined, ready . . . and dangerous.

Pulaski won the coin toss, and elected to receive. On the kickoff, they devoted two players to keeping Ronde away from the returner. Tiki squirmed this way and that, as if he were Ronde trying to get free.

But in focusing on Ronde, the Wildcats had to leave someone else unguarded. That someone turned out to be Rio Ikeda. Rio streaked down the field and threw himself headlong at the returner's legs, toppling him head over heels before he'd even gotten started!

"Atta baby, Rio!!" Tiki yelled, jumping up and down and punching the air with his fist. The game had only just started, and it already felt like the fourth quarter.

On first down, Pulaski ran the ball, but Rob Fiorilla was through the line in a heartbeat, stuffing the hole and forcing a loss of two on the play.

On the next play, Jeremy Halper threw a short completion to the sideline farthest from Ronde.

It was third and four, and Pulaski elected to pass again. This time, safety Alister Edwards wrestled the ball out of the hands of the receiver, nearly intercepting it, and forcing the Wildcats to punt.

Ronde was back there waiting for it, but the kicker aimed it across the field and out of bounds. The kick was short, but Pulaski obviously didn't care—so long as Ronde never touched the ball, they were happy.

Now the Eagle offense got to work. They gave the ball to Tiki first, just to see how far they could get.

The answer turned out to be, not far at all. Tiki was met by a wall of defenders, and pushed back for no gain.

The Eagles had known this was coming. Now it was time to launch their surprise passing attack. "Let's go to the game plan," Tiki said in the huddle.

Coach had already sent in the play—a pass to one of the Amadou twins on a crossing pattern. Tiki and Jonah would stay back to protect Hayden from the Pulaski rush. The Amadous would be outnumbered by defensive backs and linebackers. It would be up to the twins to get free, and Hayden to get the ball to one of them in mid-stride.

When Hayden faked the handoff to Tiki, the defenders took the bait. They swarmed Tiki and brought him down as if he had the ball.

From underneath the pile, Tiki could hear the roar of the crowd. When he was finally able to get up, he saw that Frank Amadou had caught the pass and taken it all the way to the Pulaski twenty-five!

"Right on the money!" Frank said as he came back to the huddle. "What a throw!"

"Nice take-out," Hayden told Felix, who had come so close in crossing Frank that the two defenders had knocked each other down, leaving both Amadou twins free.

The next play was another pass—this time, a quick one to Jonah James for a gain of ten yards.

Pulaski seemed totally off-balance. They'd assumed the Eagles would go to Tiki on most plays. Instead, they were facing an unexpectedly effective passing attack.

Hayden fired a quick square-out to Felix, and the Eagles had a first and goal at the nine.

Another fake handoff to Tiki, and this time, it was Luke Frazier who caught the quick pass. Hayden was getting rid of the ball so fast, the Pulaski pass rush had no time to get to him.

Just to keep Pulaski guessing, Coach Wheeler now called for a handoff to Tiki. It was stuffed for a loss (no one could say the Wildcats weren't ready for Tiki).

The Eagles had spent the week drilling a few very simple passing plays—plays that Hayden could master quickly, and that would cut down on the possibility of sacks and interceptions.

Now, on third and goal from the seven, Coach Wheeler called for a quarterback draw, anticipating a blitz. Hayden took the snap, faked the pass, then darted straight ahead, right past the onrushing Pulaski blitzers! He dashed into the end zone, for the first touchdown of the game!

Tiki breathed a sigh of relief, then headed over to the sideline while Adam Costa kicked the extra point.

It was going to be a long game—but at least they'd scored first. That would shake Pulaski's confidence, at least. It would take the Wildcats some time to adjust to the Eagles' simple but effective passing attack. And as long as the Eagles kept the lead, time was on their side.

The question was, could they continue to step up their game for a full sixty minutes?

CHAPTER EIGHT

AN EPIC BATTLE

THE WILDCAT OFFENSE WENT STRAIGHT TO THE run. With their huge offensive line, they were able to clear huge holes for their star running back, Curtis Drummond. Ronde could only watch helplessly from downfield. He had his man covered like wallpaper, for all the good that did.

"They're double-teaming me!" Rob Fiorilla moaned in the defensive huddle. "You guys have got to go right to the ball!"

"We're trying, yo," said Danny Halpin, one of the defensive tackles. "They're just way too big."

"And strong," Henry Weltman added. "They must have been lifting weights all week."

Whatever the reason—weights, or just the burning desire for revenge—Pulaski's offense kept on moving the chains, sticking to the ground. It was a total reversal from last week, when the *Eagles* were the ones who avoided the passing game.

Ronde could not believe how fast the Wildcats made it into the red zone. Suddenly, the defensive line that had dominated the league all season looked like a bunch of confused and demoralized rookies.

Where was all the anger and determination they'd had in the locker room? Ronde shook his head as Pulaski reeled off another nine-yard gain. Each play was different, and the blocking schemes changed each time too. The Wildcats were certainly well-coached, that was for sure.

The problem wasn't that the Wildcats had grown stronger over the past week—it was that they'd gotten *smarter*. Their coach had put in enough new plays to keep the Eagles' defense off-balance and back on their heels.

Jeremy Halper faked a handoff and ran the ball into the end zone, untouched. He let out a triumphant yell, holding the ball over his head before spiking it viciously. Then he strode over to Rob Fiorilla and yelled something right in his face.

Rob's fists clenched, and Ronde could tell he was about to do something he'd regret. "Fio!" he yelled. "Chill!"

Rob glanced at him, then turned back to Halper. But his fists relaxed. The last thing the Eagles needed was for him to get nailed with a penalty for fighting, or even thrown out of the game!

After the extra point tied it, the Wildcats kicked off—a squib kick that one of the other Eagles picked up. He was buried at the Eagle forty before he could take a step.

The Eagles had good field position, but once again,

Pulaski had managed to steer the ball away from Ronde. He could feel his frustration mounting.

"No!" he told himself as he trotted off the field. "That's just what they want—for me to get frustrated, so I do something stupid." He wasn't about to give them that satisfaction.

On the sideline, Coach Pellugi approached him. "Hey, Barber," he said, clapping Ronde on the back. "Don't get down. They've got a good game plan—we've just got to make adjustments, that's all."

Ronde nodded and sat down on the bench to catch his breath and regain his composure.

"I just told the linebackers to bunch up on the next drive," Pellugi told him. "They're going to key totally on the run. That leaves you guys in the secondary man-on-man to stop the pass. And believe me, they will pass, eventually—just as soon as they've figured out what we're up to."

"They're not gonna throw my way, Coach."

"I know that. Which is why I want you to let the safeties pick up your man."

"Huh?"

"You're going to be blitzing," said the coach.

"Every play?"

"Until I tell you different." Pellugi gave Ronde a sly grin.

Ronde returned it, and they slapped five. He liked the

idea. Sure, it meant taking a risk. If Jeremy Halper had enough time, he could find Ronde's man on a quick toss. But it was worth a try. Anything was better than staying with his man on a wild-goose chase, while Pulaski ran the ball at will.

While they'd been talking, the Eagle drive was sputtering at midfield. Hayden had thrown a quick pass so hard that Jonah dropped it. Then, on third down, the ball was deflected by a defender with long arms and very big hands.

Adam punted the ball away, and Pulaski began their next drive at the Eagle thirty-two.

Ronde's frustration was at the breaking point. But now, at last, he would get a chance to take out his frustrations on that loudmouth quarterback.

On first and second downs, the Wildcats ran again. But this time, the Eagle linebackers were able to limit the gains. Ronde knew Pulaski would have to pass on third and six—and he would be coming at Jeremy Halper for all he was worth.

The ball was snapped. Ronde ran right past the receiver, who turned in confusion when he realized he wasn't being covered.

Ronde raced right for Halper, who had his arm cocked back to throw deep. Ronde took a flying leap, and with his right hand, swatted the ball free!

He landed hard, but from the roar of the crowd, he

knew that Hidden Valley must have come up with the fumble. And it was a fumble, not an incompletion—he'd caught the quarterback's arm on the backswing.

"*That's* what I'm talkin' about!" Coach Pellugi yelled as Ronde came back to the sideline. "Now we're rollin'!"

Ronde got to watch the Eagle offense go to work. Hayden went deep on first down, just missing Felix, who was wide open, and would have scored if the pass had been on target. Next, Hayden faked a pass and rolled out, turning the corner and getting past midfield for the first down.

Tiki got the call, and ran into the usual wall of defenders. He was going nowhere today, Ronde thought, shaking his head.

He knew how his twin felt—each of them always knew—and his heart went out to Tiki. But it didn't matter in the end, as long as the Eagles won this game and survived to play another day.

On the seventh play of the drive, Hayden dropped back to pass, and the Pulaski blitz came after him. Ronde gasped as Tiki made a huge block, decking his man and causing another rusher to trip over them both.

Ignoring the pressure, Hayden reared back and threw the ball for all he was worth. Frank Amadou had a step on his man, and one step was all he needed. He reached out and cradled the ball in his fingers, then drew it to his chest without even breaking stride.

The Pulaski defender made a desperate lunge for his ankles, but Frank managed to stay on his feet all the way into the end zone. Touchdown, Eagles!

Adam's extra point made the score 14–7, and swung the momentum back to Hidden Valley. Ronde knew, though, that the Wildcats were far from beaten. They were a tough, resilient team, just like the Eagles. This was going to be a war; a slugfest; and only one team would come out of it still standing.

For the rest of the first half, the defenses held firm. The ball changed hands through a series of punts, and neither team even came close to the other's red zone.

By halftime, three Pulaski players had had to leave the game with minor injuries, and the Eagles had lost two of their own. Rio Ikeda turned his ankle making a tackle, and Frank Amadou, who took a big hit, had to have an ice pack taped to his shoulder.

Still, the Eagles had the lead at halftime, and that was important. Not that any of them thought the 14–7 score would hold up for the rest of the game. Both teams' offenses were too powerful to be held scoreless for that long.

During the break, the Eagles' coaches tended to the wounded players. Frank's shoulder was hurting, but he insisted that he could go back out and play. Rio's ankle, though, looked purple and swollen. Ronde doubted he'd be back.

That would pose a problem on runbacks, because other than him and Rio, the Eagles special teams weren't all that special.

There wasn't much talking among the players. Each of them was in his own private world. The intensity was so thick you could feel it in the air.

There were thirty minutes left in the game—and potentially, in the Eagles' season. Everything was on the line—their perfect record, their chance for a repeat State Championship—and all that separated them from disaster was a measly seven points.

Good thing we get the ball first, thought Ronde.

Pulaski kicked off out of bounds—again avoiding Ronde. After the penalty, the Eagles started from their own thirty-five. Ronde paced the sideline as the Eagles pecked away through the air, gaining a little here, a little there.

They were moving the ball, but too many of Hayden's passes were being dropped. He had a great arm, Ronde noticed, but he threw it so hard that the ball was hard to hang on to.

Just then, as if to prove the point, Frank Amadou got popped in his sore shoulder just as he caught the ball, and it flew into the air.

"NO!" Ronde screamed. But it didn't help. The ball settled right into the hands of the Wildcat safety, who ran it back past midfield to the Eagle forty-six.

Ronde grimly strapped on his helmet. *This sure isn't going to be easy,* he thought.

In keeping with the plan, Ronde kept on rushing the quarterback. But by now, Pulaski had caught on. On the first play, Ronde felt someone grab his jersey, illegally holding him while Halper threw to Ronde's man for a quick first down.

"Hey!" he yelled, spinning around and facing the kid who'd grabbed him.

"What?" the kid said, stepping right up to Ronde. "You got a problem?"

Ronde turned away, not wanting to get sucked into a fight. "He held me, ref!" he said, grabbing his own jersey to show the official what had happened.

The ref replied, "Get back to your huddles, boys. I call 'em like I see 'em, and I don't like complainers."

Ronde wanted to argue. He felt a wave of heat pass through his cheeks, but he knew it was no good.

The drive continued. Three plays later, on another blitz, Ronde was tripped and fell, allowing Halper to run around end for another first down at the Eagle twelve.

"Where's the flag, ref?" Ronde protested.

"Quit whining, son," the official shot back. "Play the game, and leave the officiating to me."

Ronde wasn't the only one steaming as the defense huddled. Several of the Eagle defenders had been tripped, illegally hit, or held on this drive.

Pulaski had started playing dirty. Ronde wondered whether their coaches knew about it, or had even told their players it was okay. He knew that none of the Eagles' coaches would ever let something like that happen. They cared about more than just winning—they cared about playing the game the right way.

The officials hadn't caught on, obviously, even though Ronde and some of the others had complained. All the Eagles were frustrated, but none of them had any answers.

On the next play, Coach Pellugi had everyone blitzing. But Pulaski was one step ahead—they called a screen pass, and when it connected, there weren't enough defenders left to keep the receiver out of the end zone. An extra point later, and the game was tied, 14–14.

On the bench, the Eagle defense fumed. "Can't call what we don't see," Henry Weltman mimicked bitterly.

That gave Ronde an idea. "That's it!" he gasped.

"What?" Henry asked.

"We've got to make sure the refs *see* it—we've got to get ourselves an Oscar for overacting, yo!"

Henry grinned, and the two of them slapped five. Soon, every Eagle defender was on board. From now on, they would exaggerate every reaction until Pulaski was made to pay for its dirty play.

The Wildcat defense, inspired by the game-tying touchdown, soon shut down the Eagles' drive, and Adam had to punt again. This time, without Rio in the game, and with Ronde double-teamed as usual, the Pulaski returner was able to get all the way to the Eagle thirty-nine.

The lead had already vanished. Only thirty-nine yards separated the Eagles from disaster. *It's now or never,* thought Ronde.

He came rushing on a furious blitz. Sure enough, Halper was in the act of dropping back to pass. When Ronde felt a hand grabbing his jersey, he wheeled his arms crazily, as if a giant claw had grabbed him, and threw himself backward onto the ground.

The pass, it turned out, was completed to Ronde's man for a touchdown. But it didn't matter, because the ref nearest Ronde blew his whistle and threw his yellow flag. "Holding, offense!" he cried. "Fifteen yards from the line of scrimmage. First down, Pulaski."

Ronde grinned as he watched the Wildcat lineman complain to the ref.

"Now you know how it feels, you jerk," Ronde muttered under his breath.

Thanks to Ronde's great idea, the Pulaski offense was suddenly thrown into reverse. On three of the next four plays, they were flagged for holding, tripping, and illegal blocks.

In every case, the Hidden Valley defender had done a whale of an acting job.

"They're faking it!" Jeremy Halper was screaming at the official. "Open your eyes, ref! Are you guys blind?"

The yellow flag flew again, this time for unsportsman-like conduct—another fifteen yards. "One more word out of you and you're ejected, okay?" the ref told Halper, waving a finger at him.

There was nothing the quarterback could do but jam his helmet back on and get back to the huddle. Ronde had to smile. It sure was satisfying to see Pulaski get what they deserved.

Soon, the Wildcats had to punt—from deep in their own end. Once again, they avoided Ronde by kicking out of bounds. But that just gave the Eagles even better field position, at the Pulaski forty-seven.

Although the offense couldn't put the ball into the end zone, they did manage to preserve the tie well into the fourth quarter. What's more, the whole game was being played in Pulaski's end of the field, which was just where the Eagles wanted it.

Sooner or later, they'd punch it in—or at least get close enough for an Adam Costa field goal.

Somehow, though, Pulaski's defense kept that from happening. With only five minutes left in regulation time, Ronde started to wonder whether they were headed for sudden-death overtime.

With four minutes remaining, the Eagles finally got close enough for Adam to attempt the field goal—but the Wildcats blocked the kick, covering the ball at their own thirty-eight—their best field position in a long while.

Ronde knew that this would be his last chance to affect the outcome of the game—unless, of course, it went to overtime. He'd been blitzing all game, and by now, the Wildcats knew he was coming. They were even calling plays where they threw to his man, knowing he'd be uncovered.

So as the Wildcats marched down the field, Ronde began to panic. Something had to change, or Pulaski was going to grab the lead.

"Yo, Justin! Alister!" The Eagles' other corner and free safety came over to him.

"What's up?" Alister said.

"Listen, Al—you've got to cover my man from the get-go," Ronde told him.

"But then, what happens if Justin's man gets free?"

"Justin's not gonna let that happen. Are you?" Ronde asked him.

"I've got him covered," Justin said. "Count on it."

"Okay, but . . ." Alister didn't sound convinced.

"Trust me," Ronde said. "They're gonna throw at my guy, not his. They won't see you coming. Just be ready."

On the next passing play, Ronde came at Jeremy Halper full-tilt.

WHAM!!

He was hit square in the back—an illegal block. Ronde hit the ground, seeing stars. There was no acting this time. There was no flag, either.

But because Alister had covered Ronde's man, Halper had no place to throw. Rob Fiorilla sacked the Wildcat QB for a ten-yard loss!

Now it was third and fifteen. Ronde knew it would be another pass play. If the Eagles stopped this one, they'd get the ball back with time to notch a winning score.

Ronde lined up at his usual spot. Then, on the snap, instead of going straight at the quarterback, he slid toward the center, then cut unseen through a hole in the line.

Halper was looking the other way, toward his number one receiver, whom Alister was covering. The quarterback never saw Ronde coming.

Ronde hit him just as he was throwing. The ball shot straight up into the air . . .

. . . and into the hands of Rob Fiorilla!

The burly Eagle defensive end seemed shocked that he was holding the ball—but he snapped out of it in a flash, and started running for all he was worth.

"Go, Fio!!" Ronde yelled, jumping up and down. "GO!!"

Fiorilla was tackled at the Pulaski thirty. There were three minutes left in the game, and now it was the Eagles who had the last, best chance of winning in regulation.

Ronde could only stand and watch as the Eagles' offense took over. Hayden handed off to Tiki, who fought through the mob of defenders and dragged two of them down to the twenty-two.

But then the Wildcat defense held firm, batting away two straight passes.

It was Costa time. Adam trotted onto the field, looking calm and collected. Ronde grinned. Nothing ever rattled that guy—at least not on the football field. Sure enough, he split the uprights, giving the Eagles a 17–14 lead with just two minutes left to play.

Pulaski got a big runback out of the kickoff, and started out near midfield. They surprised the Eagles with a run on first down, and Ronde gritted his teeth as the officials spotted the ball at the Eagle thirty-eight.

Another ten yards and the Wildcats would be in range of a tying field goal.

He couldn't let that happen! He *wouldn't*.

On first down, he blitzed, doing a complete 360 to avoid the running back's block. He slammed into Jeremy Halper only a second after he got the pass off. Lying on top of the Pulaski QB, he heard the roar.

He sprang up to see Justin Landzberg running with the ball! Because of Ronde's pressure, Jeremy Halper had thrown an interception!

Justin was brought down at the Eagle forty, and the crowd went wild. Eagles' players hugged one another and jumped up and down. With only thirty seconds left, they'd just cemented their biggest victory yet!

That's when Ronde felt something hard bump into him.

"You guys cheat!" Jeremy Halper was yelling at him. "You stole this game!"

"Stole, nothing," Ronde shot back, yanking off his helmet. "We won it fair and square. You're the ones who played dirty."

Next thing he knew, Ronde felt Jeremy's fist crashing into his cheek. "OW!" he cried, stumbling backward.

Ronde saw red. Everything was blotted out, except the strong urge to hit Halper back.

"RONDE!" came a loud voice behind him—a voice he knew as well as his own.

Tiki put a hand on his shoulder. "It's okay, man. It's *over*. We've got them beat. Don't take a stupid penalty now!"

Ronde forced himself to swallow hard and contain his fury. Looking around, he saw the officials trying to separate other players who were yelling at one another. Apparently, he and Jeremy weren't the only ones close to fighting.

No flags were thrown in the end, because the only punch thrown had been by Halper, and the officials had missed it.

The teams lined up, Adam kicked a squibber. The returner was buried by a half dozen Eagles, and the final gun sounded!

In the midst of the giddy celebration, Ronde saw Jeremy Halper slamming his helmet to the ground.

Ronde felt a twinge of embarrassment. He'd let the kid get away with hitting him.

Still, he was glad he hadn't punched Halper back. It could have cost the Eagles the game, or more probably, gotten Ronde suspended for the Eagles' *next* game. And that would have been too high a price to pay for the pleasure of getting even.

Tiki was right. Fighting never solved anything, anyway.

Ronde shook off the bad feelings and dove headlong into the wild celebration on Hidden Valley Field.

CHAPTER NINE

THE CAPTAIN'S BURDEN

COOTIE HARRIS WAS THE STAR OF THE BIG PEP rally held that Saturday evening at the school gym. The Eagles' mascot did flips, somersaults, and cartwheels, and led the bleacher creatures in Eagle cheers and songs.

Tiki and Ronde weren't new to pep rallies. There'd been one last year too, on the way to their state championship. But to Tiki, the rally he liked best was the one *after* they'd brought home the trophy.

Rallies like this one, *before* they'd even won the *league* championship, could only jinx a team. If they went on and won, great, but it was what everyone expected. If they *lost*, though . . .

Tiki thought back to the mirror breaking over Thanksgiving. He knew it was supposed to mean bad luck. He also knew that was just a superstition. But where did superstitions come from, he wondered? How did they get started? There must have been a real case of bad luck, way back in the day, for people to start talking about it, right?

And the mirror hadn't been the end of things either. Ronde's lucky penny went missing the week after, and twice, Tiki's path had been crossed by a black cat.

"Hey, Tiki . . ."

"Huh? What?" Tiki stared up into Cootie's concerned face.

"You okay, dude?"

"Y-yeah. Why?"

"'Cause you look kind of spaced-out."

"No, no, I'm okay, man. I'm fine. Fine!" He smiled and nodded to show that he was just as excited as the rest of them. Cootie, satisfied for the moment, turned away, back to the business of working up the crowd.

Soon, Tiki fell back into his own private thoughts. Manny had been knocked out of his quarterback spot for the last two games. They'd somehow managed to win without him. But just today, Manny had told them he was still on the disabled list—doctor's orders.

So Hayden Brook was going to be the man again, for the third game in a row. *Well, at least he has some big-game experience now,* thought Tiki, looking over at Hayden.

The kid looked confident, all right. He was already being treated like a star by most of the kids in school—especially his fellow eighth graders. Three cute girls surrounded Hayden now—two of them cheerleaders. Hayden was beaming with pride.

Tiki suddenly had a sinking feeling—one he'd had

before. Sure it was good to be confident—but Hayden looked *way too* confident.

North Side had a record of 11–1, and they'd done it all with their defense. The Rockets had a ferocious pass rush and good cover guys. Hayden would really be up against it this Wednesday.

Tiki thought of the broken mirror again. Was the bad luck Manny going down? If so, it hadn't hurt the Eagles—yet.

Monday at lunch, the team's tables in the corner of the cafeteria were mobbed with people. Hayden was holding court, telling everyone about certain plays in the Pulaski games—plays featuring heroics by *him.*

He wasn't bragging, exactly, Tiki thought. He sounded humble, saying how scared he was when those big guys were coming at him—but *still . . .*

Two girls were holding up a banner that said, EAGLES— STATE CHAMPS AGAIN!

That did it. Tiki felt the anger rising inside him as he went over to them and said, "Put that thing away."

"Huh?"

"Why?" The two girls looked disappointed, but they lowered the banner and started rolling it up. "What's wrong with it?"

"We're not state champs again, that's what's wrong with it," Tiki said. "We're not even league champs yet. All you're gonna do with that is jinx the team."

The two girls looked hurt, and Tiki felt sorry he'd said it in such a mean way. But he still thought it was wrong to act like champs before you were champs. Wrong—and bad luck, too.

"Hey, give 'em a break, Tiki," Paco said. "Everybody knows who the best team is. Right, yo?"

A cheer went up from everyone around.

"Maybe so," Tiki said. "But we've still got to win the games."

"Oh, yeah," Rob Fiorilla said, grinning and nodding. "That's right."

"We're gonna stomp North Side," Cootie said, holding his arms skyward, as if he were the one who was going to do the stomping.

Tiki laughed and shook his head. Cootie had to weigh in at about 120 pounds—in *shoes.*

"Those Rockets are gonna fizzle!" Justin Landzberg said, making a raspberry sound that had everyone cracking up.

Tiki shook his head again. This was more than he could take. If he couldn't stop them all from crowing, he didn't want to be here.

Turning his back on the celebration, he went to the food line, got his lunch, and ate alone in a far corner of the cafeteria.

He didn't really blame his teammates for feeling good—no, not good, *great.* They'd come through, minus their star QB, against Pulaski, their archrivals—twice in a row. They had every right to crow about it—especially the young ones who'd stepped up to the plate when the Eagles' stars were neutralized.

Tiki didn't want to spoil their good time—that's why he'd sat at this empty table, far away from "Eagle Corner."

He didn't know why he felt so anxious. Was it really the broken mirror and the black cats? Or was the constant pressure starting to get to him?

He was well aware that he'd run for only twenty-three yards in the last game against Pulaski. Was he losing his magic touch? Or was it the curse of the broken mirror?

North Side's D was even better than the Wildcats'. How was he going to be able to carry his team to the League Championship?

It didn't make it any easier that everyone was counting on him.

He thought about Ronde. Where *was* his twin, anyway? He hadn't shown up at lunch yet.

Tiki wondered if Ronde was feeling the same sense of impending doom. . . .

That night, both Tiki and Ronde had to study for finals. They sat at the kitchen table, papers and books strewn all around them.

It didn't help. Neither boy could really concentrate on his schoolwork.

"Where were you at lunch?" Tiki asked.

"I was studying," Ronde said. "In the auditorium."

"Really? Since when do you ever do that?"

Ronde sighed. "Well, I didn't really want to come to lunch and sit around yukking it up with the guys and all," he explained.

"Yeah, I know what you mean." Tiki was not surprised that Ronde shared his distaste for the strutting and goofing around. This was a serious time for all of them—or it should have been, anyway.

"What's gonna happen with Hayden if things start to go wonky against the Rockets?" Tiki wondered.

"I don't know," Ronde said, shaking his head. "He's gone a little off the deep end, hasn't he?"

It wasn't really a question, so Tiki didn't bother to answer.

"You know," Ronde finally said, "he's a pretty good player. He can be as good as Manny, in his own way."

"Manny's a proven gamer," Tiki said. "That counts for something, even though it doesn't show up in the statistics."

"True." Ronde tapped a book rhythmically with his pencil. "Well, we'd better get back to work."

"Yeah . . ."

Neither boy did, though. They were still talking football when their mom came home from work at nine o'clock. They were so absorbed in conversation that they didn't even say "hi."

"Are you all talking football?" she asked, dropping her bag on the floor and putting her hands on her hips. "Is that what you call studying?"

"Aw, Mom," Ronde said. "It's too hard to concentrate, with the big game coming up on Wednesday."

"Too hard to concentrate?" she repeated. "What about your big test you've got Tuesday—as in, tomorrow?"

"Ronde's right, Ma," Tiki said. "We've been trying, but it's impossible!"

"Let me remind you boys of something you might not want to hear," she said, leaning against the counter wearily. "Do you see how tired I am? I worked two jobs today, just to make enough to pay the rent here and put food on the table and clothes on our backs."

Tiki and Ronde looked down at the table. Tiki knew his mom worked hard. He wished she didn't have to work two jobs, that she could make enough from just one job to support the family.

"I want you boys to get good grades and go to college," she said. "Grades are more important than championships. A championship is nice to remember years later— but good grades lead to making a better living for the *rest* of your *life*. Do you understand what I'm saying?"

"Yes, Mom," they both answered.

"Good. Now get back to your books—and don't give me any more of this 'impossible' nonsense."

Tiki and Ronde knew she was right—but right now,

grades didn't *feel* as important as a championship. Nevertheless, they both finally got down to it, and managed to really study for an hour before bedtime.

That hour of study helped them get B's and A's on all their finals, and on Wednesday they marched into the locker room together feeling pretty good about themselves.

That feeling disappeared when they saw how their teammates were acting before the big game.

Three of them were throwing water at one another out of paper cups, laughing and giggling. Two others were play-wrestling.

"Yo!" Tiki yelled.

"Tiki!" they all greeted him. "Ronde! Yo!"

"Hey, settle down, you guys," Ronde told them.

"Yeah, we've got a game to get ready for," Tiki added.

"This game is in the bag!" Alister Edwards said. "We've got Rio back, dudes!"

Rio Ikeda grinned, showing them his ankle, which was wrapped in an ace bandage. "No limping!" he reported, giving them a thumbs-up.

"And we've got Manny for the regionals!" Justin told them. "His doctor just gave him the okay to play."

That really was good news, Tiki had to admit—*if*, that is, the Eagles *got* that far. First they had to win today's game against North Side. And the Eagles seemed to think it was going to be an easy victory.

Fine, so long as they got out to an early lead, thought Tiki. But what if they didn't? How would the Eagles react if their confidence got shaken?

Because of the Eagles' perfect regular-season record, all their league play-off games were at home. That was a good thing, mostly, in Tiki's opinion. You could feel the crowd behind you, and when the other team had the ball, they did their best to drown out the quarterback's signal calls.

But if you messed up on the field, doing it in front of a home crowd made it even worse—you could feel their disappointment, their agony (your own times two thousand!), their frustration.

It had happened to Tiki and Ronde in the course of their three seasons at Hidden Valley. It happened to *everyone* sooner or later—especially the team's "skill" players: receivers, running backs, defensive backs, and especially *quarterbacks*.

Tiki remembered Cody Hansen last year, messing things up more than a few times, and then making things worse with his attitude. Cody had finally come around, just in time for the Eagles to go all the way to the State Championship.

Now it was Hayden Brook's turn. From their first offensive possession, things started going wrong, and it only went downhill from there.

Hayden muffed the first snap of the drive—luckily,

Luke Frazier fell on it. Then he threw the ball ten yards too far, missing Felix Amadou by a mile. On third down, he seemed to panic when the blitz came, and stood there frozen instead of scrambling. The result was a sack, and the Eagles had to punt.

That first drive was only the beginning. By the time the first quarter was over, Hayden had turned the ball over three times—two interceptions and a fumble on a rollout. He was carrying the ball far from his body—an easy target for slapping away.

Tiki felt like his head was about to explode. The Eagle fans were on the edge of booing Hayden, and Tiki could see that the young QB was shaken. He seemed close to tears, his former confidence totally gone.

For his part, Tiki had done his best. His carries had resulted in thirty-seven yards for the Eagles, but it hadn't amounted to anything, because Hayden kept making mental mistakes.

The rest of the Eagles were starting to grumble among themselves. One or two of them had even lost it—Paco groaned, "Oh, come on, man!" when Hayden committed the fumble.

Tiki felt the same as Paco, but he knew it was no use to complain to Hayden—that would only make things worse, killing whatever shred of confidence the kid had left.

The Eagle defense, led by Ronde and Rob Fiorilla, was

doing its best to keep North Side at bay. But when the other team gets the ball on your side of the field every time, it's hard to keep them out of the end zone. The score was already 10–0, and as a result of Hayden's latest fumble, the Rockets were threatening again.

Normally, Coach Wheeler would have called Hayden to the bench and sent in his replacement. But the Eagles had no "Plan B"—Manny was out, and there was no third-string quarterback. Rio Ikeda was listed that way on the roster, but as a seventh-grader, he hadn't taken a single snap, and there was no way he was going into a play-off game.

"Coach," Tiki said, approaching Wheeler. He'd stayed silent as long as he could, but he had to say something to somebody. The game was rapidly getting out of control. If things kept up this way, it would soon be impossible for the Eagles to come back and win.

"What's up, Barber?" Coach Wheeler said, without turning away from the field. His eyes looked haunted— but so did the eyes of every Eagle and every Eagle fan. This was not what anybody had expected—not even in their worst nightmares.

"Coach, put me in at QB!" Tiki urged him. "I can do it—and the team needs me."

Wheeler glanced his way and let out a bitter laugh. "Are you nuts?" he asked. "We need you doing what you do best."

"But Hayden—"

"Hayden's a good player," Wheeler said, glancing down the bench at his quarterback, who was sitting there staring at the ground. No one sat within six feet of him. It was as if he had the plague. "He's just down right now."

"Well, can't you talk to him? Get his spirits back up?"

"I've already tried," Wheeler said, sighing. "It didn't seem to do much good." Then he looked at Tiki. "Maybe if his *captain* said something to him . . ."

"Me?"

Coach Wheeler shrugged. "Sometimes it means more coming from somebody your own age. Somebody who's been there himself, not too long ago."

Tiki nodded, and went slowly over to sit down beside Hayden. "Hey," he said.

"Hey," Hayden replied, without looking up.

On the field, North Side broke a long run. They were in the Eagle red zone again, with a first down at the twelve yard line. Tiki winced.

"Listen," he said, putting a hand on Hayden's back. "This game is not over."

"No?" Hayden said bitterly. "I don't know about that."

"Hey—no matter how bad you feel right now, you've still got time to turn things around. Remember, you're the same guy who won the last two games for us."

"Uh . . . in case you forgot, there were a bunch of other guys who helped win those games too."

"And those guys are right here with you now!" Tiki said, jumping on any opening Hayden gave him. "We're all ready to stage a huge comeback. We just need you to take charge!"

"I think the guys are pretty steamed at me," Hayden said, wincing. "I can't blame them. I'm stinking up the joint."

"Forget it—it's in the past, dude. We've got three quarters—well, two-plus quarters—left to make up a measly ten points."

Just then, the Rockets threw a touchdown pass that Ronde narrowly missed batting away. The crowd groaned. Hayden looked down at the ground again.

"Make that seventeen points," he said, even before the extra point was notched.

"Look, just keep to those few simple pass plays we've got down," Tiki told him. "Let's take it one score at a time, okay? If we can hang onto the ball from here on in, we can beat these guys! We've beaten them twice already this year, and we scored forty-two points both times!"

"That was with Manny at QB," Hayden reminded him.

"Dude," Tiki told him, "you can *do* this. *WE* can do this. Just forget what's already happened, stick to the game plan, and hold on to the ball. In fact, give it to *me* a few times to start us off. I'll get us some field position, and then you can do your thing."

Tiki patted him on the knee and stood up to get back on the field.

Hayden rose to his feet. "Tiki," he said, "I don't know if—"

"*You can do this*, kid," Tiki cut him off. "I've been in your shoes, more than once, and I *know* what you're going through. I'm telling you—*you can do this.*"

Hayden took a deep breath, blew it out, and nodded, his jaw set firmly and his eyes burning with intensity. "Okay, let's go," he said. Not waiting to see if Tiki was following, he ran out onto the field, clapping his hands together, all fired up.

"Geez, what did you say to him?" Paco asked as they jogged toward the huddle.

"Tell you later," Tiki said, grinning. "Let's play some football!"

CHAPTER TEN

BACK FROM THE BRINK

"ATTAWAY, TIKI!!" RONDE YELLED. HIS VOICE WAS drowned out by the general noise of two thousand fans screaming their heads off. Tiki had gotten the home fans excited with three straight runs for big gains.

North Side was throwing everything they had at Tiki, but it didn't matter—he just would not go down.

Of course, the Eagle offense couldn't just keep handing the ball to Tiki. He already looked exhausted, and why not? He'd been dragging defenders on his back play after play. The Eagles were on the North Side twenty-seven, but now they were going to have to try something else.

Hayden dropped back, then flicked a quick pass to Luke Frazier. It happened so fast, and the ball got to Luke so quickly, that there was no time for the defense to react.

It wasn't a difficult throw for Hayden, and the pass rush had no time to put pressure on him. In short, it was exactly the kind of play Hayden could succeed at, and Ronde knew that every successful play—no matter how small the gain—would add to Hayden's confidence.

Confidence was everything, Ronde knew. Up until

now, the Rockets had had the Eagles doubting themselves—especially Hayden. Now that the Eagle offense
was moving, Ronde could feel the momentum shifting.

He watched as Tiki took the ball again, and drove it
down to the five yard line. Ronde could barely contain
his excitement. The Eagles were about to score a touchdown, he was sure.

Then it would only be a two-touchdown lead. It was
just the first half. The Eagles had come from even further
behind this season, so there was no need to panic.

Except for one thing: The defense was going to have to
stop North Side cold. They'd already given up seventeen
points, but that was because the Rockets had started deep
inside Eagle territory due to Hayden's mistakes.

The Eagles could not afford for their QB to keep fum-
bling and throwing the ball away. He seemed steadier
now, throwing another quick pass to Luke at the three.
On third down, Coach Wheeler called a rollout.

Felix Amadou was covered in the end zone, and the
linebackers weren't fooled by the fake handoff to Tiki.
They stayed with Hayden, and brought him down at the
five yard line. The Eagles had to settle for a field goal that
made the score 17–3.

"Well, we've gotta do what we've gotta do," Ronde said
to himself as he strapped his helmet on. For the Eagles to
win, he was going to have to make a big impact on this
game—starting right here and now.

The Rockets started their next drive at the thirty yard line. With a two-touchdown lead, they tried to eat up the clock by keeping the ball on the ground. But the Eagles were ready for them, and soon it was third and long.

Here came the pass play, Ronde knew. They'd probably try to keep it simple—a quick throw to avoid the blitz, just long enough for a first down.

Ronde gave his man a hard bump, sending him reeling backward. Then he headed for the forty yard line, which was exactly how far the Rockets needed to get with the pass.

Sure enough, their halfback had sneaked through the Eagle defensive line and now turned quickly to receive the throw. But Ronde was there first, leaping in front of him to grab the ball out of the air for the interception!

It was exactly the break the Eagles needed. No sooner was the offense back on the field than Coach Wheeler called a pass play—this time, going straight for the end zone. And Hayden, suddenly feeling it, threw a perfect strike to Frank Amadou in the corner of the end zone for the touchdown!

By halftime, the score was 17–10, Rockets. But everyone in the Eagle locker room was focused and ready. Nobody crowed, or bragged, or fooled around, or even talked much. They were a bunch of men on a mission.

It wasn't life or death, of course—but it might as well have been. Ronde saw the looks in their eyes, and inside his heart, he *knew*—this team was not going down in defeat. Not today. Not this game. *No way.*

As Ronde waited for the second half kickoff to come down into his arms, he tried to still his pounding heartbeat. "Breathe," he told himself. "Breathe . . ."

He took the ball and squeezed it hard to his chest, making sure he had a good grip before he began to run. Somehow, he felt an extra sense of alertness. It was like everyone else was moving in slow motion.

Starting with a stutter step that made two rushers trip over themselves and tumble to the ground, Ronde darted this way and that, spinning away from one tackle, ducking under a leaping rusher, and finally finding a seam of daylight.

That was when he kicked it into high gear. Two more defenders skidded to the ground, grabbing for his legs but ending up clutching nothing but air. Ronde's legs whirred at amazing speed, and everything turned red in his vision as he raced for the end zone!

He felt hands grab his ankles just as he crossed the goal line. Clutching the ball even tighter, he hit the ground hard, but kept possession. Touchdown, Eagles!

The crowd went nuts, and the band launched into a victory march, with the big bass drum pounding. Adam raced onto the field, and his extra point was true, as usual.

Tie game, 17–17! And after the Rocket offense went three and out, it was the Eagles' offense turn.

Ronde couldn't wipe the grin off his face as he stood on the sideline. With the great runback he'd given them, the Eagles had all the momentum now.

Gone was the shaky, tentative, scared quarterback who'd gotten them into the hole. *This* Hayden Brook was playing out of his mind—having the game of his life (or at least the second half of one!). He was throwing pinpoint short passes to Tiki, Luke, and Jonah, mixed in with an occasional long toss to one of the Amadou twins.

North Side's defense was on its heels, panicking. Ronde could see it in their body language. Some of them were yelling at their teammates who'd been caught flat-footed. Turning on one another.

Ronde had seen that kind of behavior before—even among his teammates—when things went wrong. It was never a good thing.

Before the Rockets could make any adjustments, the Eagles had racked up another score, on a mad twenty-yard sideline dash by Tiki.

It was Ronde's turn again. This time he contributed a thundering sack on a blitz, forcing the Rockets to punt after only three plays.

By the fourth quarter, the score was 31–17, Eagles. The Rockets had the ball, but now, fourteen points behind with only fifteen minutes to play, they had to go to their passing game.

Coach Pellugi put an extra defensive back out there—Rio Ikeda. That made it possible for one of the five to rush the quarterback on every play, and still cover the receivers man-to-man.

With so much pressure on him, it was only a matter of time before the Rockets' quarterback made a mistake. Seeing that his other receivers were covered, he threw it to Ronde's man—something most teams had avoided doing all season, and with good reason.

Ronde, a step behind, easily made up the lost ground once the ball was in the air. He leaped at the last minute to make the interception, then avoided being brought down by the receiver.

With the ball in his hands, in the open backfield, it was like running back a kickoff. Once again, Ronde shifted into that extra gear he'd had ever since his growth spurt.

He was all over the field, running toward one sideline, then doubling back toward the other, only to spin back inside and dart down the center of the field, blazing all the way to the end zone.

He was going so fast that he had to keep going, right up the stairs of the bleachers. Some of the home crowd grabbed him so he could stop himself. They clapped him so hard on the back that he said, "Ow!"

The Eagles were rolling now, and they never looked

back. The final score was 45–17—a complete rout of the demoralized Rockets! The final ten minutes was a rollicking, loud celebration by the Eagles and their fans, cheering for the League Championship they so richly deserved.

Hayden and Ronde got game balls from Coach Wheeler. Ronde saw Hayden give his to Tiki, along with a big bear hug.

Ronde knew Tiki had said something to Hayden when the kid was falling apart in the first quarter. He didn't know what it was, but it sure had done the trick.

Whether Manny came back for their next game or not, the Eagles now had a quarterback they could rely on from here on in. Someone they could ride—hopefully—all the way to the State Championship!

CHAPTER ELEVEN

PLAY-OFF BOUND!

TIKI HOISTED HIS BOOK BAG OVER HIS SHOULDER, left his last-period math class, and headed down to football practice.

Tiki was happier than he'd been in a long time. For one thing, he'd done well on his big tests—which meant that he could take it easy for the rest of the term. All his teachers were in holiday mode too. The vacation was less than two weeks away, and most of the serious teaching was over until January.

But that wasn't the only reason Tiki was feeling light. The Eagles had won the League Championship, keeping their perfect record intact. Even if they lost in the Regionals, at least they would have accomplished something great—something no one could take away from them, ever.

He and Ronde would graduate and go on to Hidden Valley High, but they'd never be forgotten. Their photos would be on the wall outside the gym, holding up all those trophies and awards they'd won. Kids years from now would try to live up to their achievements.

It was a great feeling. But there was still much more to accomplish. And if they won their next three games, they would reach the greatest goal of all—a repeat State Championship, with not a single loss in the whole season to spoil the perfection of the achievement.

The cherry on top was, the Eagles now had Manny back the rest of the way. His scrambling ability, and his feel for the game, were better than any QB Tiki had played with so far. With Manny behind center, it would be a huge boost for the Eagles.

All this time, he'd had to worry about their chances. Now, at last, he felt good about things. That broken mirror, and those black cats, were just a thing of the past. The Eagles had weathered the storm, he was sure.

That is, until he arrived at practice, and heard what Coach Wheeler had to say.

"Okay, listen up, offense," Wheeler began, putting one foot up on the bench and balancing his playbook on his knee. "Manny's back—but he still has to be treated carefully. That means he won't be practicing with us, except for noncontact drills. Nobody comes near him, got it?"

Tiki frowned. He got it, all right. But without real repetition, complete with the defense going after him, it would be hard for Manny to get back his rhythm.

"I'm going to give Hayden lots of reps," Wheeler went on, "because if Manny gets hit during the game, and has to sit down, we're going to need Hayden to be ready.

"I'm also putting you offensive line guys on notice—you too, running backs—that your number one job on pass plays is to keep your quarterback from getting hit. Now, let's go over the plays for our game with Loudon. . . ."

Tiki could barely focus on the rest of Coach Wheeler's talk. The thought of Manny hitting his head on the turf again gave him the shivers. The Eagle defense might take it easy on him in practice, but it was up to Tiki and the offensive line to protect Manny against Loudon's pass rush. And that, he knew, was not going to be any picnic.

The Loudon Giants were 13–1, counting the play-offs in their league. They were as fast as the Eagles, even if they weren't quite as big. And they had home-field advantage, because this year it was their league's turn to host the regional play-off.

This was the Eagles' first away game in five weeks. They'd gotten used to having the home crowd behind them. So it was weird to run out onto the field, yelling at the top of their lungs, and not hear the crowd roaring with them.

That roar was reserved for the Loudon Giants. When they came running out, fast as a stampede of horses, their fans went wild. Tiki winced, thinking how hard it would be to hear Manny's signal calling with all that racket.

"How're you feeling?" Tiki asked his quarterback as they paced around on the sideline. "You ready for this?"

"Ready as I'll ever be," Manny replied, shrugging.

"Gotta get my feet wet first, then we'll see. Hopefully, I won't get hit too hard."

"You're not going to get hit at *all*," Tiki promised. "I've got your back, Manny. I'll be sticking to your blind side, just in case they come at you that way. Count on it."

"Thanks, dude," Manny said, clapping Tiki on the shoulder. "Hey, I'm not worried – as long as we've got you to carry the offense, my job's a breeze."

They slapped five, and ran out onto the field for the coin toss. When it went up, Manny called heads—and heads it was.

A good start—but from there on, things didn't go so smoothly for the Eagles. Ronde gave them pretty good field position with his runback, and Tiki got them eight yards on first down. But on Manny's very first pass play, the ball sailed high, and right into the arms of the Giants' free safety!

"Don't worry, yo," Tiki told Manny as they walked off the field together. "You're just a little rusty. Stay with it, and you'll find the range."

The Eagle defense bent but didn't break. After eight plays, the Giants tried a long field goal—and missed.

"See?" Tiki told Manny as they strapped their helmets back on. "No harm done. Just put that throw behind you, and let's go get 'em!"

But on their second drive, the same thing happened. Manny threw a third-down screen pass, but the ball floated too much, and the Loudon cornerback was able to get between the ball and the receiver. He came down with it, and this time, Loudon drove the ball into the end zone with a series of quick passes and a mad dash by their quarterback, for a 6–0 lead after the extra point.

On their next drive, Coach Wheeler had the Eagle offense go to the ground game—specifically, to Tiki. The Giants' defensive line was smaller than Pulaski's or North Side's. And fast as they were, they were no match for Tiki's hyperdrive speed and quick moves. He tore them up for fifty-two yards—and that was just on the ground. Manny also found him with a quick buttonhook pass in the end zone to nail the touchdown!

Adam's extra point tied the game, and that's the way it stayed until just before halftime. With a minute left on the clock, Tiki got the Eagles into the Giants' red zone with a long run, breaking away from two tackles along the way.

Then, on the last play of the half, the Eagles pulled a double reverse—Manny handed off to Tiki, who ran toward the sideline, then handed off to Luke, who was going in the opposite direction. Luke turned the corner and dove into the end zone, stretching the ball out in front of him—touchdown, Eagles!

The halftime score was 14–7, and things were looking good. Other than scoring off the interception, the Giants hadn't shown much offensive power, and they had yet to find a way to stop Tiki.

. . .

The second half began with surprises, and none of them was good. On the kickoff, Loudon's return man lateraled the ball to one of his teammates, just as he was getting tackled by Ronde. The second guy made it all the way to the Eagle thirty before he was brought down.

From there, the Giants pulled a stunt play on first down: a flea-flicker. It began the way the Eagles' double-reverse had in the first half. The quarterback handed off to the running back, who handed it to the fullback going the other way. But the Giants added another twist—the fullback lateraled it back to the QB, who launched a bomb into the end zone!

Ronde had been fooled by the reverse, and found himself chasing the fullback, bringing him to the ground just after he'd tossed the ball back to his quarterback.

The receiver in the end zone was free to make the grab for the touchdown. The extra point went up—and just like that, the score was tied again.

From there on, it was a tight game. Tiki kept on racking up the yards, and Manny found his passing rhythm again. The Eagle blockers were picking up the rush, just like Coach Wheeler had told them to, and Manny was not being hit—not at all.

Still, the Giants were able to keep the Eagles out of the end zone. Whenever Tiki and his teammates got into the red zone, the defense stiffened and got really stingy.

The Giants clogged up the middle, and had the speed to defend runs around end. Twice, the Eagles had to settle for short field goals. Once, they tried to run it in on fourth down, but Luke got stonewalled at the goal line.

On the other side of the ball, the Giants were moving the chains, but they weren't doing much scoring either. They notched one touchdown via the run, but Ronde stopped another long drive with an unbelievable interception in the end zone.

Late in the fourth quarter, with the Giants leading by one measly point, but driving again, Ronde made the play of the game. On third and long from the Eagle 40, the Giants had to pass. Ronde came on a corner blitz, hitting the quarterback just as he was about to let go a long bomb to a wide open receiver in the end zone.

The ball came loose, flew straight up, end over end, and Rob Fiorilla grabbed it! He lumbered toward the Giants' end zone, and Ronde got up in time to throw a key block, freeing Rob to make it all the way to the Giant twenty!

The clock was winding down. Only thirty seconds left in the game. But it was the Eagles who held the ball—and they were already in field goal range.

Tiki took the handoff from Manny on first down and drove to the eleven yard line. Now they were down to twenty seconds, and Coach Wheeler called the Eagles' second time-out.

"I want you to throw to the end zone on second down,"

he told Manny. "If it's incomplete, we go to Tiki on third down. If that doesn't work, we call our last time-out, and send Adam out to nail the winning field goal."

The pass on second down was on target—but Felix Amadou let it bounce right off his chest. Felix went down on his knees and grabbed his head with both hands, roaring with frustration as the crowd's cheering drowned him out.

It was Tiki's turn on third down. He took the handoff and blasted through a hole in the line created by Paco, who bulled over the nose tackle like he was made out of paper.

Tiki streaked forward, willing himself into the end zone for the winning score. . . .

THUNK!

The next thing he knew, he was on the ground, staring up at his teammates who were bent over him, their helmets in their hands.

"What happened?" he asked.

"You okay, Tiki?" Paco asked, looking worried.

"You got *hit*, dude," Luke told him.

"What?"

Tiki suddenly realized he wasn't holding the ball.

"It's okay," Luke told him. "We recovered the fumble at the fifteen."

"But the clock—!"

"Coach called time," Paco said. "There's one second left. Adam's gonna kick it through, don't worry. Here, let me get you up," he added, thrusting out a hand for Tiki to grab.

"Don't touch him!" Coach Wheeler's voice cut through everything. He nudged Paco and Luke aside and knelt beside Tiki.

"How many fingers am I holding up?" he asked.

Tiki squinted. He couldn't really tell. Was he seeing double?

"Uh, four?"

"That's it," Coach said. Turning, he called over his shoulder, "Bring the stretcher!"

"What? No, I'm fine!" Tiki insisted, though his head was throbbing. He tried to sit up, but the whole field started spinning, and he laid back down.

As they carried him off the field, he could hear the polite applause of the Giant fans.

"I'm fine, I'm telling you!" Tiki kept saying as they brought him to the sideline. "Let me watch the kick!"

They stopped the stretcher long enough for Tiki to watch Adam put the game-winning field goal through the uprights.

"Yesss!" Tiki said, thrusting his fist into the air. "OWW!!" His head throbbed like mad, and he grabbed it with both hands.

"Okay, let's get you to the locker room," said Coach Wheeler.

There, lying on the stretcher, surrounded by his happy, tired, but worried teammates, the doctor examined Tiki, who was already feeling a little better. His headache had calmed down some, and he was no longer seeing double.

"It's a mild concussion," the doctor told Coach Wheeler. "Not as bad as Manny's."

"Oh, great," said Coach Wheeler, letting out a relieved breath. "I thought—"

"But still," the doctor interrupted, "no football for ten days."

The words hit everyone like a sledgehammer—but they hit Tiki hardest of all.

Ten days? *He'd miss the team's next game!*

"But Coach—!" he started to protest.

"No buts, Barber," Wheeler said, putting a hand on Tiki's shoulder. "Doctor's orders. We're just gonna have to find a way to win our next game without you."

A groan went up from the assembled Eagles, and Tiki buried his head in his hands.

This could not be happening! Not to *him*—not *now*!

Ronde sat down and put an arm around his twin. "It's okay, Tiki," he said. "We've got this. We are not going to go down, I guarantee it."

The players filed out, but Tiki sat there, still as a statue, feeling like he wanted to burst out crying. "Coach," he begged at one point, "let me play next week—I'm already better! I'll be fine, really!"

"Barber," Wheeler said, sitting on Tiki's other side, "let me tell you about a guy I played with in college, back in the age of the dinosaurs."

That made Tiki smile, but only for a second.

"This guy was some kind of football player—a running back, like you. Well, he got hit hard one day. It was a concussion—'a mild one,' the doctor said. Just like yours. But that guy played his next game—and guess what? He got hit again. It was the end of his career. He never played competitive football again."

Tiki looked up at Coach Wheeler, who was staring right into his eyes.

"Now, I don't want that to happen to you, Barber. You've got a real future in this game, and you can't forget about that. You can't let your desire to win now be more important than the rest of your life. And I don't just mean in football. Concussions are serious things. Your future is far more important than any championship."

He got up, took a few steps toward the door, then turned back to Tiki and Ronde. "And guess what?" he said. "I believe we're gonna win it anyway."

He smiled, winked, and walked out of the locker room, leaving Tiki and Ronde behind to think about it.

"He's right, you know," Ronde finally said.

"I'm fine!" Tiki insisted. "Why doesn't anybody believe me?"

"No, I mean about the game," Ronde said. "We *are* gonna win. We're gonna win it for *you*, Tiki. No doubt about it."

CHAPTER TWELVE

OUT ON A LIMB

RONDE HAD FELT AFRAID BEFORE IN HIS LIFE— plenty of times. Once he'd seen a rattlesnake—right in a neighbor's backyard. The snake shook its rattle at him and stuck its tongue out. He didn't remember screaming as he ran away, but Tiki'd always sworn he had.

Ronde wasn't embarrassed about it, even if he had screamed. Rattlesnakes are poisonous, after all. Sometimes, it's good to be afraid, he thought—because it helps you stay alive and healthy.

But it was definitely not good to be afraid before a football game—especially the Western Regional Final against the Abingdon Angels.

And yet, somewhere deep inside, a germ of pure fear was eating at Ronde. He couldn't seem to wish it away, or think it away, or distract himself from it. Playing a team that was every bit as undefeated as the Eagles was enough of a challenge. Doing it without Tiki was going to be crazy hard!

Ronde had even gone to Coach Wheeler and offered to play running back as well as his own position. "I can do it, Coach!" he insisted. "I know all the plays. Tiki and I run them together all the time, in the street in front of our house."

"I'm sure you do, Ronde," Wheeler had said, giving him a sad smile. "But I need you at full strength on defense and special teams. If we're gonna win this game, we're gonna have to do it as a team. Every player is gonna have to step up and play the game of his life—not just you."

"But it's more important for us to have a good running back than a good defender!" Ronde blurted out.

Coach Wheeler frowned. "Where did you get *that* idea?" he said sharply. "And do you really believe that? What you do for this team is every bit as important as what your brother does. How many times have you saved our bacon? How many interceptions? How many runbacks for touchdowns?"

Ronde looked down, embarrassed. He hadn't meant it that way—it was just that Tiki was so important to the Eagles . . .

"I need *both* you guys—you *and* Tiki—to be captains to the rest of these kids. I want you both to keep everyone else focused, in the locker room and on the sideline, and to let me know when somebody needs a breather. Got me?"

"Yes, Coach," Ronde said. And that was the end of the discussion.

. . .

Now, as he prowled the sideline, waiting for the game to begin, Ronde had to get his own fear under control. Because if *he* was afraid, so was every other player on the Eagles! And as captain, it was *his* job to help them conquer that fear—so he had to conquer his own first.

"Just play your game, like you do every week," he told himself. "Don't hold back. Play proud. Win it for Tiki." He repeated those few simple phrases over and over again, willing himself into game-readiness.

The whistle blew. The teams took the field. Tiki, in uniform but with no helmet, paced the sideline like a caged tiger. He yelled himself hoarse, clapping his hands in encouragement.

Ronde took the kickoff, and was quickly surrounded and brought down. He came off the field, and told Tiki, "They're fast, and strong. We've got to make those blocks right the first time, or they're going to eat us alive."

Tiki nodded, and went over to speak to some of the special-teams blockers. Unable to play, he could at least be an extra coach, giving the players whatever extra attention they needed to raise their game.

Abingdon had a record of 14–0, same as the Eagles. Unlike the Eagles, they hadn't had a single close contest all year. Ronde had seen their record, printed in that week's *Roanoke Reporter*. The Angels' stats were intimidating. Clearly, they had good special teams, and Ronde now got a chance to watch their defense at work.

Without Tiki, the Eagles had inserted Rio Ikeda at running back. Rio had run all the plays several times in practice—but since he was smaller and thinner than Tiki, Coach Ontkos abandoned the power runs, concentrating instead on the sweeps that took advantage of Rio's speed.

On second down from the Eagles' forty-three, Rio got loose, and fooled three different defenders with moves Ronde didn't even know he had.

"Wow!" Ronde said, clapping as Rio came off the field for a breather. "Where'd you get those moves?"

"Born that way, baby!" Rio said, grinning. "Just give me a chance, and watch me do my thing!"

Okay, Ronde thought, shaking his head and smiling. So what if Rio was feeling a little cocky? It couldn't hurt to have confidence, as long as he continued to back it up.

The Eagles got close enough for Adam to fire off a field goal, getting them on the board first at 3–0. The Abingdon crowd sat silent, stunned. It was only the second time all year that the Angels had trailed in a game.

Ronde trotted onto the field, ready to chase down the kickoff returner. The kick was high, and shorter than Adam's usual effort.

By the time it came down, Ronde was right there. He nailed the return man so hard that the ball came loose. Another Angel covered it, but Ronde had made his point. Today would not be another easy victory for Abingdon!

On offense, the Angels looked like a well-oiled machine. While they didn't pull off any spectacular plays, they advanced steadily on the ground, and with short, quick passes. Ronde found himself out of the action. That frustrated him, but at least he was no longer afraid.

Abingdon was a good, well-coached team, for sure. But so far, they hadn't done anything dazzling. Nothing like a 14–0 team, anyway.

Maybe it isn't that they're so good, Ronde thought. *Maybe their league is just weaker than ours.* Had the Angels' opponents been a bunch of pushovers . . . ?

"Maybe we can beat these guys after all," he muttered under his breath, even as the Angels kicked a field goal to tie the game at 3–3.

Back on offense, Ronde and Tiki both shouted their lungs out cheering, as Manny fired three straight pinpoint passes to three different Eagle receivers.

After a Luke Frazier burst for a first down at midfield, Manny went back to work again, finding Felix Amadou at the twenty-seven, then his twin, Frank, at the fourteen.

"Man!" Ronde said, grinning at Tiki. "I don't think I've ever seen him this good."

"He's playing his guts out," Tiki agreed happily. "My man, Manny! Yeah!"

Manny faked a long bomb, then tucked the ball under his arm and dashed right into the end zone! The Eagles whooped and hollered, pumping their fists. Tiki turned to Ronde as the extra point went up and said hoarsely, "I'm already losing my voice!"

On the next drive, Abingdon's best receiver faked a square out and went long on first down. Ronde had seen this move before, thanks to Coach Wheeler and his belief in watching video of the other team's games.

Ronde knew the play would be coming, knew it would be on a first-down play, and knew exactly when to turn back and look for the ball.

It was almost as if the QB had thrown the pass to Ronde. He came down with it, still in stride, and made a quick loop back up the field.

"Now catch *these* moves!" he muttered under his breath, showing Rio, the Angel defenders, and everyone else what he could do with the football in the open field. He dodged, deked, double stutter-stepped, and sped all the way into the end zone—touchdown, Eagles!

Another extra point, and the Eagles held a comfortable 17–3 lead. The first quarter ended and the second began, but it was more of the same story. Ronde intercepted another pass, and then Manny pulled off a dazzling drive, scrambling and pinpoint-passing the Eagles to another touchdown.

The game was 24–10 at the half, and only because of one long bomb the Angels completed because Ronde was tripped—a case of offensive pass interference that the referees didn't spot. Ronde protested, but he knew enough to back down before he drew a stupid penalty.

"Take it out on the field," he told himself. "Play smart. We're in the lead. Don't say anything you'll regret later."

In the locker room at halftime, the talk was all about Abingdon, and how they were a paper tiger—a team with a record they could never have put up against teams like Pulaski, North Side, and Hidden Valley.

Tiki had lost his voice completely, but he looked pretty happy. Antsy too. He couldn't stop pacing the floor.

"Chill out, bro," Ronde told him. "You're gonna wear out your sneakers."

"I can't relax," Tiki said in a hoarse whisper.

"Why not? We're winning. We're playing our game. What is there to worry about?"

"I don't know. It's just . . ."

"What?" Ronde said. "Are you thinking about that broken mirror again?"

Tiki nodded.

"Just forget it, man! It's a stupid superstition."

"That's what I thought, and now look at me," Tiki whispered. "It didn't take but one hit to knock me out of this game."

Ronde frowned. "Stay positive, Tiki. The bottom line is, here we are. We haven't lost all year, and we're not gonna lose today, either."

"I sure hope not."

"Hey—I guaranteed it, didn't I?"

Tiki flashed him a weak smile. "Go get 'em, cowboy."

The bad break Tiki feared was not long in coming.

On their first drive of the half, Paco went down with a badly twisted ankle. Without him in their way, the Abingdon pass rush suddenly got a lot better. Manny's scrambling staved off disaster, but the Eagle offense started moving backward instead of forward.

In the meantime, the patient Abingdon offense was getting their team back in the game. Staying away from Ronde now, they went back to the combination of short passes and power runs to wear down the Eagle defense. By the time the fourth quarter rolled around, it was 24–20, and the Angels were driving again.

This time, they threw a long pass at Justin Landzberg's man, coming across the middle. Justin made a great leap to knock the ball away, but he landed on his wrist, and immediately grabbed it, wincing in pain.

With Justin out, the Angels had more success passing. Alister Edwards moved from his safety position to cover Justin's man, but Abingdon's tight end and running backs were getting free for short passes that soon brought the Angels to the Eagle ten.

Ronde could see the look in their eyes. It said, *We're*

winners! We're unstoppable! No team has ever beaten us, and no team ever will!

"Oh, yeah? That's what you think," Ronde muttered as he took his position opposite the Angels' premier receiver. Bumping his man out of the play, he sped right for the quarterback, who was looking around for someone to throw to.

Ronde leaped into the air and deflected the pass. It landed in the arms of Alister Edwards, and that was the end of the Angels' drive!

Deep in their own end, the Eagles' offense went to work. Manny ran the ball himself twice in a row, scrambling for a total of eighteen yards. Then he found Rio on a quick screen.

The Eagles kept churning out the yards, taking up a good chunk of time. Finally, they were forced to try a field goal from the twenty-one yard line. But one of the Angels burst through the center hole, where Paco would normally have been, and blocked it.

Even worse, he landed on Adam's leg! When the Eagles' all-star kicker got up again, he was limping.

"Oh, no!" Ronde moaned. That made four key Eagles who were out of the game. With five minutes left to play, could the defense stop Abingdon one last time?

The Angels' strategy was to run the ball, using up all five minutes of clock, so that the Eagle offense wouldn't get possession again. It was a gamble—a field goal wouldn't be enough, so they'd have to score a touchdown. But Abingdon's coaches obviously felt they could do it.

And why not? They'd only scored two TDs, but they'd moved the ball well all day.

There was nothing Ronde could do about it. No sense rushing the quarterback if the Angels were running the ball. He had to stay with his man, just in case, so he was not available to help stuff the runs that kept coming, tiring out the Eagle defense.

Ronde noticed that Rob Fiorilla was sucking air, his hands on his hips, bending over to catch his breath.

Ronde pointed to him, and to the sidelines, signaling Coach Pellugi to send in a replacement. Rob was a great player, but he was out of gas. The Eagles needed fresh blood on the D-line to stop the relentless Angel running game.

With under a minute left, and Abingdon at the Eagle seventeen yard line, Ronde started to feel the panic rising inside him. He knew it was the same for every Eagle defender. Their whole season depended on keeping Abingdon out of the end zone right here.

The only thing going for the Eagles was that they had less ground to cover in the backfield now that Abingdon was so close to the end zone. It meant the Eagles' backs could bunch up near the line of scrimmage. That made it harder for the Angels to run straight at the Eagles' line. Their drive slowed, and the Angels had to spend their time-outs.

With twenty seconds left, it was third down and goal to go at the four yard line. Both teams were out of time-outs now. If the Angels ran, and didn't get into the end zone, the clock might run out before they could run another play.

That meant they'd be throwing for sure. Ronde only hoped he got a crack at the ball. Surely, the Angels would go to the opposite side of the field.

Thinking along the same lines, Coach Wheeler called for a safety blitz. Alister charged through a gap in the line, chasing the quarterback out of the pocket. Now all the receivers had to abandon their original patterns and try to get free.

Ronde followed his man toward the center of the end zone.

The Abingdon quarterback ran first toward one sideline, then the other, desperately trying to find a target. Since there was no daylight between him and the goal line, he couldn't take a chance on trying to run the ball in for the winning score.

He could either run out of bounds, saving a precious few seconds for one last play, or he could fire the ball at one of his receivers, knowing that if they dropped it, the clock would stop.

All he had to do was make sure the ball wasn't picked off. He fired it low, so that it couldn't be knocked up into the air, a free ball for anybody to snag.

What he didn't see coming was Ronde Barber.

Quick as lightning, Ronde dove low, reaching out one hand and grabbing the ball just before it fell into the hands of the receiver. He held the ball against his helmet as he fell, keeping it off the ground. Somehow, he didn't lose control of it.

The whistle blew, and the ref signaled interception!

Five seconds later, after Manny took a knee, the game was over!

The Eagles had handed Abingdon its first defeat. Ronde and his teammates were Western Regional Champions—make that *undefeated* Champions—and they'd done it with Tiki on the sideline!

"What did I promise you?" Ronde exulted as he hugged his twin. "What did I say?"

"You did, you did," Tiki admitted.

"Never mind those silly superstitions," Ronde said. "They've got no power over us—we are Eagles, bro!"

It was only when they arrived in the visitors' locker room that they got the bad news: All three of the Eagles' wounded—Justin, Paco, and Adam—would be out for the State Championship game!

"Man," Ronde breathed, suddenly joyless. "Tiki, you'd better be back for that game, or everything we've done so far is going to go up in smoke."

CHAPTER THIRTEEN
THE MISSING MEN

TIKI AWOKE WITHOUT A HEADACHE. That made it three days in a row now. He'd already forgotten what it was like to wake up with them. Thank goodness he'd been cleared to play by the doctors!

The big game was tomorrow morning, and he felt like his old self again. Later, after school, he and the rest of the Eagles would board their bus for Richmond. They would sleep in dorms at Richmond University, same as last year. And tomorrow, the Eagles would take the field to defend their crown against mighty Richmond Prep.

Most of the Eagles, that is.

Adam Costa, their all-world kicker, would miss the big game with a sprained ankle. That meant the Eagles could forget about field goals. They'd be going for two points after every touchdown as well.

Once before, during last year's regular season, they'd been forced to play without Adam, and Tiki had filled in. The Eagles had survived, but just barely. Tiki would have to do the kickoffs and punts tomorrow, but he wouldn't be kicking for points. *No way.*

The team would also be without Paco Rivera, their all-league center. At the moment, his left ankle was in a soft cast. Without him, would Manny be protected from the Richmond Prep pass rush? Would the snaps go smoothly—especially the long ones on third down, and to Tiki on punts?

As if that weren't bad enough, Justin Landzberg, the team's other cornerback, was down with a broken wrist. Rio Ikeda would substitute for him, but that just made the Eagles' pass defense thinner and weaker.

The three injured Eagles would travel with the team, and cheer them on from the bench—but that was all they could do, against a Richmond Prep team that was coached by former NFL players, ranked number one in the entire Southeast—and, of course, undefeated.

So even if Tiki's own headaches were gone, he and the Eagles still had plenty of headaches to deal with.

It was the last Thursday before Christmas. After the game, there would be no school for almost two weeks! By the time the new year rolled around and classes resumed, the football season would be history.

If the Eagles won, of course, there would be a celebration planned in the gym or the auditorium, and the whole school would turn out to cheer their football heroes.

If they lost, though, the whole season would be a painful memory. It would be ancient history, and everyone would try to forget the miserable way it had ended—so close and yet so far! *If only those three key players hadn't been injured*, they'd say, and shake their heads. A perfect season, ruined.

Well, not altogether—they'd still be League Champions for the third year in a row, and Western Regional Champs two years running.

Tiki remembered, back when he and Ronde were in seventh grade, riding the bench for the Eagles. That year, the team had lost in the State Semifinals. Quarterback Matt Clayton, who'd been the big hero of the school up to that point, had pretty much disappeared all that spring. Now he was a star in high school, but his fame at Hidden Valley Junior High was over the minute the Eagles lost that game.

Would it be the same for Tiki, Ronde, and the rest of this year's team?

No, Tiki reasoned, it would be *worse*—because this year, everyone was *expecting* them to win. If they didn't— well, he didn't even want to *think* about that. They *had* to win. They just *had* to!

That night, he and Ronde were sharing a dorm room. It was almost lights-out time when Ronde said, "Hey, let's go hang out with Paco and those guys. They're probably feeling like crud on toast."

"Good idea," Tiki agreed.

They walked down the empty hallway. Most of the

doors to the dorm rooms were closed. The team members were tired—it had been a long trip to Richmond. But the door to Paco's room was open.

Inside, he, Adam, and Justin sat silently, their faces wearing identical expressions of misery.

"Hey, guys," Tiki said. "How's it going?"

Paco looked up from the floor. "How do you think?"

"This stinks," Adam said, then sighed wearily. "I don't know why we even bothered to come here. It's just gonna be torture to watch us get killed."

"Hey!" Ronde objected. "Who says we're gonna get killed?"

"Face it," Justin said. "Without Adam, how are we gonna keep up with those guys? They score, like, forty points a game or something. Adam's our biggest scorer."

"Hey, what am *I*, chopped liver?" Tiki asked.

"They're not scoring any forty points off *us*," Ronde vowed. "I guarantee you that."

"I don't know," Paco said, shaking his head. "It just seems like we've been pushing our luck for the past six weeks. Maybe this is the last straw. Maybe our luck has finally run out."

Tiki swallowed hard. The image of the broken mirror flew into his mind's eye. The black cat crossed the path of his imagination.

He shook his head violently, to get the images out of his mind. Luckily, even that didn't give him a headache, or he would have wound up kicking himself for being so stupid as to shake his head hard after a concussion.

"Listen, you guys," he said. "We're a *team*. One or two of us—or even three—can go down, and the rest of the team can step up and take over for them."

"Even Adam?" Justin asked. "Who's gonna kick field goals for us? *You*?"

Tiki had no answer for that one, but luckily, Ronde stepped in.

"Yo, listen up," he said. "None of us would have gotten this far without all the rest of us pulling for him."

He looked each of the stricken players in the eye, then added, "We've come all this way. And we are *not* going back home without that trophy. You hear me?"

One by one, all three injured Eagles nodded. Ronde put out his hand, and they all covered it with one of their own. "Go, Eagles!" they shouted together, not caring whether they woke up their teammates.

It was a cold but sunny day that Friday, as the teams took the field for the State Final. Tiki scanned the packed stands, filled with more than ten thousand people from all over the state. TV cameras were everywhere—the game was being broadcast on local stations throughout Virginia.

Tiki knew that his mom was not in the stands. Although she came to nearly every one of their home games, and many of their road games too, she could not take the day off from work to travel all the way to Richmond. She worked at two jobs. Once, she'd even held *three* jobs at the same time!

Tiki knew that, even at work, she'd have a TV rigged up somewhere, somehow, and would be checking on the game every chance she got.

He forced himself to refocus. It was important to not get carried away by the huge crowd and all the media people. You still had to focus on your game, and especially on your opponent.

Tiki thought back to what Coach Wheeler had told them in the locker room. "The Renegades have won fifteen straight games this year," he said. "They didn't do it by being soft, or slow, or weak, or dumb. They did it the old-fashioned way—they *earned* it. They averaged forty points a game, and gave up an average of only sixteen.

"But look at it this way—*so what? We've* won twenty-something straight games, dating all the way back to last year's regular season!"

A cheer went up from the Eagles—even the three who were injured.

"So I hope there's no fear in this room," Wheeler went on. "There shouldn't be. We're missing some of our best guys, sure—but each and every one of you has had your heroic moments this season. All we have to do is bring that same intensity to *this* game. If we do, we'll win—and that's a *promise*."

Another cheer rocked the walls of the locker room. Several of the Eagles pounded on the metal locker doors for added effect.

"We're gonna have our hands full," the coach continued. "They're bigger than we are, and probably stronger. Definitely richer and better-equipped." This got a laugh from the assembled players. "But we're *faster*—remember that. And in spite of the fact that they've got great coaches, I say we're *smarter*!"

The cheering got even louder, and only died down a little as Wheeler finished his speech:

"Besides, look at all the ups and downs we've been through together. If we focus our energies as a team, for just one measly little hour, we can walk away State Champions, with a perfect season we'll all remember for the rest of our lives!"

"Holy jumpin' Hannah!" Rio said as the Eagles stood on the sideline and watched the Renegades run onto the field. "They're even bigger than they looked on video!"

"I didn't know they made Junior High School kids *that* big," Tiki said, shaking his head. "What are they feeding them, anyway?"

The Renegades roared, made pumped-up muscle poses, and threw one another around, just to show the Eagles how strong they were.

It *was* a little intimidating, Tiki had to admit. But he

didn't care how big or strong they were. The Renegades were not going to steal the State title he and the Eagles had worked so long and hard to win.

The coin toss went to Richmond Prep, and Tiki lined up to kick the ball. He had to concentrate really hard because, due to his concussion, he hadn't practiced with the team all week. In fact, this was the first kick he'd tried since last season—and he hadn't been very good back then!

Still, it wasn't too bad a kick. Luckily, it took a big Eagles bounce, then hit off one of the Renegades, but was smothered by another before the Eagles could steal it.

On their first drive, Richmond Prep tried to go straight to the passing game. But either they hadn't seen any videotape of recent Eagle games, or they were ignoring the blitz.

Ronde came at them on second down and nailed the quarterback so hard, the kid had to come off the field for a breather.

The Renegades wound up having to punt, and Ronde was ready again. He ran the kick back to the Richmond Prep twenty-five!

Tiki ran onto the field, excited by the way the game was going so far. With all his heart, he believed the Eagles could win this game, even without Adam, Paco, and Justin.

He took the handoff on first down, and blew down two defenders on his way to a twelve yard gain! On the next play, he took a short pass from Manny and ran it to the four.

Then it was Manny's turn. He faked a handoff to Tiki,

turned, and ran around the far corner for the touchdown!

The two-point conversion went to Tiki, who powered it in, staying on his feet even though he was in the grip of a huge linebacker.

When he kicked off for the second time, it was with a lead of 8–0.

Within twenty seconds, it was 14–0!

Ronde slammed into the return man so hard he let go of the ball, and it fell right into Rio's hands. Rio turned on the jets, and was into the Renegade end zone before anyone could react. The two-point conversion failed this time, but the Eagles had Richmond Prep on the run, and they weren't through yet!

By the end of the first half, the Renegades' quarterback had been sacked four times—twice by Ronde and twice by Rob Fiorilla. Tiki had run for another touchdown, and the score was Eagles 22, Renegades 3.

"We've got this game!" Rio exulted as they got to the locker room. "This baby is *over*!"

Tiki winced. He was as happy as any of them, sure, but he knew better than to count any game over before the final gun sounded.

Besides, there was still that broken mirror to overcome. . . .

CHAPTER FOURTEEN

BY THE SKIN OF THEIR TEETH

Although he would never have told anybody—not even Tiki—deep in his heart, before the game started, Ronde couldn't help having the feeling that the Eagles were going to lose.

He would have been thrilled if the score had been tied at halftime. But to be ahead by nineteen points, against the *Renegades*? And without three of their key players?

No way. He had never imagined it would turn out like this, and neither had any of the others.

The Eagles were soaring, full of joy and confidence. To Ronde, they looked like world-beaters. Richmond Prep looked off-balance, back on their heels.

Coach Wheeler glared angrily at his players. "Hey!" he yelled, in that piercing voice of his. Everyone fell silent at once.

"To listen to you all, you'd think the game was already over!" He gave them a second glare, going slowly from one end of the locker room to the other.

"We've got thirty minutes of football left to play. You guys haven't achieved *anything*. Not yet. And if you keep carrying on like this, maybe you never will. Now settle down, and focus on what you *personally* need to do in the second half."

He took off for the men's room, and the murmuring started right away. "Bummer," Manny said, shaking his head. "I don't know why we shouldn't be happy right now."

"It's not that," Tiki said. "He just wants us to keep our edge."

"That's right," Ronde said. "Richmond Prep is not just gonna sit there and take their medicine."

"They'll make adjustments," Tiki explained. "So we've got to be ready. In fact, we should be one step *ahead* of them."

Everyone nodded, and there was more murmuring, but this time, it was in a tone of agreement.

"If we win this game," Ronde said, "there'll be plenty of time for celebrating."

The second half started with a bang, and quickly turned into an all-out war.

Sure enough, the Renegades had revamped their entire game plan. Now they were running—but not just up the middle. There were rollouts, and reverses, and double reverses.

Soon they had Ronde and the rest of the Eagle defense totally out of breath. By the time they finally threw a pass, their receivers had an easy step on the cornerbacks—including Ronde. For the first time in months, a man Ronde was covering beat him for a touchdown!

Ronde couldn't believe it. He grabbed his head with both his hands and screamed in frustration.

The Renegades tried for two, and made it, plowing over the defensive line. Rob Fiorilla and his linemates were back on their heels now, and looked just as off-balance as Richmond Prep had in the first half.

Ronde took the kickoff, determined to make up for his mistake. He fought his way through careening rushers to almost midfield.

The Eagles ran behind Tiki, and got as far as the eight yard line before the drive petered out. Without Adam, though, they were forced to throw on fourth down, and tight end Jonah James dropped the ball in the end zone.

Back in possession of the ball, Richmond Prep stayed on the ground. They ate up almost the whole third quarter with their next drive.

Every time the Eagles had the Renegades stopped, they found a way to keep the drive going. It took sixteen plays and twelve minutes, but in the end, they crossed the goal line for the score.

The Eagles lined up for the two-point conversion, and the Renegades executed a direct snap—a trick play where the center snapped it right to the running back, who threw a completion in the end zone to a wide open receiver!

Ronde threw his hands up in the air and groaned. "Whose man was that?"

"Yours, dude," Justin told him.

"Mine? But—" Dang! Justin was right, Ronde realized. The receivers had crossed paths, and Ronde had gotten himself mixed up.

The Renegades were right back in the game, trailing by only a field goal, 22–19, with a whole quarter of football left to play. And the Eagle defense had suddenly lost its mojo.

Why? What had happened to suddenly sap their momentum? Was it the early celebrating at halftime? Or was it Coach coming into the locker room and bringing the Eagles down off their cloud?

Either way, it had to stop, Ronde realized as he lined up to take the kickoff. *Somebody* had to make a big play for the Eagles, or the Renegade wave would break right over them, and wash the Eagles' whole season out to sea!

Ronde took the kick and ran for all he was worth. Sheer speed and force carried him past the initial rushers. Two quick shuffle-steps in succession got him past two more, and then he was running again, right down the sideline, before being crashed into at the Renegade thirty-five.

The Eagle offense was set up beautifully. Ronde had given them the break they needed. But without Paco at center, snapping the ball like clockwork, blocking the pass rush, and blasting holes for Tiki to run through, the team was having a tough time gaining ground.

Manny kept scrambling. Once, he even lateraled to Tiki to avoid being tackled for a loss. That play turned into a big gainer—but still, the Eagles came away without a score. With no field-goal kicker, and a rookie center, they lacked their usual offensive punch.

The Renegades took over at their own three yard line. Ronde was determined to keep them bottled up in their own end of the field. After all, the Eagles still had the lead. If they stopped Richmond Prep cold, victory would be theirs!

The Renegades stayed with the run, blasting holes in the exhausted Eagle line. Rob Fiorilla was blowing out breaths and holding his hands on his hips, and Coach Wheeler waved him off the field, sending in a seventh-grader as a replacement.

Richmond Prep ran right at him, and gained another twenty-five yards before Ronde brought the running back down.

Now the Renegades were at midfield. So much for keeping them in their own end!

Rob Fiorilla came trotting onto the field again. He'd had only a minute to catch his breath, but the team needed him—just like it needed all its big guns when it came to crunch time.

Ronde could only hope the Renegades would try to get cute and throw a pass. If they kept running the ball, they were going to get at least into field-goal range. The only good thing was that time was running down. The Renegades had only one time-out left, and with all those running plays, the clock had never stopped.

If the Renegades scored, and went on to win this game, Ronde knew he would never forgive himself. It was *his* lapse that had led to Richmond Prep's last touchdown, and the following two-point conversion, too. If the Eagles lost, it was on *him*, and no one else!

This is no time for regrets, he told himself. *It's time for* redemption!

He knew the whole Eagle defense was playing on tired legs. He himself was exhausted, panting and sweating bullets as he lined up opposite his man.

The quarterback handed off to the halfback—but instead of running with it, he threw up a pass—to Ronde's man!

Ronde could hardly believe his luck—those high-powered coaches at Richmond Prep had just outsmarted themselves! Pushing his burning legs to the limit, he raced after the pass, leaped into the air . . .

. . . and brought it down for the interception!

It was the play of the game, no doubt about it. Ronde clutched the ball like it was his newborn baby, only giving it up when the official pried it from his hands.

He staggered off the field as the offense trotted back on. He couldn't even manage to lift his hand to be high-fived!

Manny, Tiki, and the rest of the offense ran down the

clock, keeping possession as long as they could—but it wasn't long enough. They had to kick the ball away with thirty seconds left—and Tiki, pressured by the rush, muffed the kick!

The Renegades took possession on the Eagle forty, with twenty-four seconds still to play, and one time-out still in their pocket.

Ronde couldn't believe it! He'd thought they'd already won!

He'd been so sure the offense could run out the clock on Richmond Prep. But now he had to get back out there, and stop the desperate Renegades one more time.

"Barber!" Coach Wheeler barked at him. "You stay here for one play, and catch your breath."

"No, Coach, I—" Ronde began, but Coach held out the palm of his hand to stop any further complaints.

By the time Ronde got back into the game, the Renegades were at the Eagle thirty—almost close enough for a field goal that would tie the game. If that happened, and it went to overtime, there was no way the Eagles could win.

Their offense was going nowhere against the bigger, stronger Renegades. And the Eagle defense was *done*. *Exhausted*. Finished for the day.

Overtime would mean a sure loss.

They had to hold here, Ronde knew. On third down from the twenty, with ten seconds left, he blitzed the quarterback, thinking it might be a pass.

He missed, but he managed to turn the QB the other way, where he ran smack into Rob Fiorilla. The sack, the Eagles' fifth of the day, sent the Renegades back to the twenty-eight. Close enough for a field goal, but only just. Richmond Prep called their last time-out with only one second left on the clock.

Ronde knew from reading the *Roanoke Reporter* that the Renegades' kicker was the best in the state. If anybody could make this kick, under this kind of pressure, it was him.

But if anybody could stop him, it was *Ronde!*

Taking a running start as the ball was snapped to the holder, he ran straight at Rob Fiorilla, who was bent forward and low. Ronde climbed right up Rob's back and jumped up from there, his arms stretched out as far as he could manage.

THWACK!

The kick hit him square in the left palm, and shot straight into the air! It came down into the hands of the kicker, who was buried by Eagles as the final gun sounded!

"VICTORY!!" Ronde screamed, thrusting both fists in the air. Then he let himself drop backward onto the ground, gasping for breath, but smiling wider than he ever had in his life!

He lay there, watching his exhausted teammates hug one another, fall to their knees, cry, laugh, shout, and dance.

Ronde felt so much love, for so many people—his mom, his brother, his coaches, his teammates, every kid and teacher at Hidden Valley Junior High—the list went on and on.

At that moment, Ronde Barber loved the whole wide world!

The team returned home to Roanoke at seven in the evening. The buses were greeted by over two thousand cheering Eagles fans—students, teachers, local residents, and of course, Mrs. Barber, who was right up front, holding a big sign that said, WELCOME HOME CHAMPS!!

There were hugs all around, and finally, the boys all went off in their separate directions.

As Ronde settled into the backseat of their old station wagon, Tiki talked nonstop to their mom about everything she'd missed—from the dorms, to the meals in the cafeteria, to the play-by-play of the big game.

Ronde already knew the story. He sat silently, watching the streets go by as they rode to the restaurant where Mrs. Barber was taking them out for a big dinner to celebrate. Restaurants were expensive, but this was a rare occasion.

Ronde thought back to the moment of victory, and the celebrations that followed as soon as everyone recovered from their exhaustion.

It had been a grueling game—a hard, long, grueling

season, in fact. Ronde felt bone-tired. He had no idea where Tiki was finding the energy to work his mouth so fast and for so long. It made Ronde smile.

Then he thought of what tomorrow would be like. It would be hard to go back to normal life, without a big game to prepare for.

There would be the long Christmas break, and that would be fun. Then there would be a whole term of school. Tiki would go back to writing his advice column in the school paper, and Ronde had promised to help him with it.

Why had he done that, anyway? Ronde frowned, but he knew there was no way out of it. Besides, he was good at giving advice—maybe even better than Tiki. But nothing would be as good as the two of them doing it together.

That was the main thing. To stay together as a family, and as brothers, all through life, no matter where it took them. Ronde stared at Tiki yammering to their mother, and he thought, *I have the best brother and mother on the planet.*

After dinner, after they'd gone home and their mom had settled on the couch to watch the late night news, Tiki turned to Ronde and said, "I'm not tired. You?"

"Nuh-uh."

"Want to go for a walk?"

"*Now*? It's past ten o'clock."

"So what? Tomorrow's Saturday. And we're on vacation, yo."

"Where are we gonna go?"

"You'll see," said Tiki with a grin. "Come on. Mom, we'll be back in an hour, okay?"

Ronde followed his twin outside, down Amherst Street, and then up the dirt path that led into the open field behind the houses. Suddenly, he knew where Tiki was leading him.

"Our old fort!" Ronde said, grinning.

"How long has it been since we came here?" Tiki asked as they came to the mound of dirt and rocks that had always been their secret place.

"More than a year," Ronde guessed.

"At least."

The stars were out, and it was still warm for December. "Nice out here," Ronde said.

"Yeah. Today was incredible, huh?"

"Outstanding."

"Super-excellent!"

"Supremo!"

They both laughed, and exchanged the handshake.

"We've done it, man," Tiki said. "Everything we dreamed about before the season started."

"Can you believe we actually went *undefeated*?" Ronde pointed out. "I mean, that might never happen to either of us ever again."

"Tell you the truth, I thought when we broke that mirror, it was all over."

"I told you it was just a superstition," Ronde said.

"*What*? *I* was the one who told *you* that!"

"Aw, now, come on—don't change the story."

"Facts are facts, son."

Again they laughed. Who cared which of them was right? It was ancient history, and it just went to show that superstitions were dumb.

"We played our game, didn't we?" Ronde said.

"We did, we did," Tiki agreed. Then he sighed.

"*What*?"

"Huh?"

"What are you thinking?"

"Oh, about the future," Tiki said. "The far future, I mean."

"Oh."

"I mean, do you think we'll really go all the way to the NFL?"

Ronde looked his brother in the eye. "No doubt."

"Yeah? It's *tough*, Ronde. Not many people get there, no matter how hard they dream."

"You know what?" Ronde said. "Even if they don't get where they planned, they get *somewhere*. It's not *wasted* time, you know? You get a lot out of it when you try that hard at anything."

"You know what? You're right," Tiki said, patting Ronde on the shoulder. "I sure am glad you're going to be writing my advice column for me next term."

"*What?*"

Tiki was laughing. "Just kidding, bro."

"Better be!"

"But you are going to help me, right?"

"Dude, you *need* help. I can't leave you there to fall on your face."

"What?"

"Just kidding."

It was like old times, the two of them horsing around together. Ronde felt lighter than he had since the season first began.

Looking up, he saw the neon star on top of Mill Mountain. "Our lucky star," he said, pointing.

"You know," Tiki said, "we're not always going to come out champions, Ronde. Nobody wins *all* the time."

"Doesn't matter," Ronde said. "I mean, even if we'd lost today, it *still* would have been worth everything we put into it."

"We gave it one hundred percent," Tiki said, nodding.

"And that's *never* a mistake."

Ronde put an arm around his twin's shoulder. "You know what? Whatever the future holds for us, we're gonna be ready. Because you've got *my* back, and I've got *yours*."

"And Mom's got *both* our backs," Tiki said. "Man, are we lucky, or what?"

They headed back home, not wanting her to worry about them.

Ronde was totally on top of the world, even if it was only for this one night. Whatever the future held, at least he and Tiki now knew what it took to be winners, on the field and in life:

Whatever you did, you had to give it one hundred percent of your effort, all the time—heart, mind, body, and spirit.

Whatever you did, you had to *play proud.*

WHERE DID THE NFL TEAM NAMES COME FROM?

ARIZONA CARDINALS:

In 1994 this team was renamed the Arizona Cardinals, with a red cardinal on the uniforms, although the name does not relate directly to the city like some other teams. The team became the Cardinals when Chris O'Brien bought jerseys from the University of Chicago and declared the color "Cardinal Red."

ATLANTA FALCONS:

In 1965 Julia Elliott was picked to give the team name for Atlanta. She said, "The Falcon is proud and dignified, with great courage and fight. It never drops its prey. It is deadly and has a great sporting tradition." Now, the Falcons are represented by an aggressive looking Falcon, which is oddly shaped as an F.

BALTIMORE RAVENS:

The Ravens' team name and logo were chosen in fan contests. They were to pay tribute to the raven in the famous poem "The Raven" by Edgar Allan Poe, who lived in Baltimore.

BUFFALO BILLS:

The public was left in charge of picking a name for this team, so they went with a name that was used before by a team in the All-American Football Conference, the Bills.

CAROLINA PANTHERS:

The Carolina Panthers represent both North and South Carolina. So, when the Panther was chosen, the Panther's head was shaped to look like the borders of both states.

CHICAGO BEARS:

Because of the popularity of their baseball team the Chicago Cubs, owner George Halas decided on the Chicago Bears, with a "C" for Chicago on the helmet. But, he liked his own school's uniform colors, orange and blue, so much that he used those colors for the Chicago Bears.

CINCINNATI BENGALS:

Owner Paul Brown wanted a way to connect to the past. He used the name Bengals because of the many past football teams who had the same name. Instead of taking the color of a Bengal, which is white, he used the colors of his former team in the logo.

CLEVELAND BROWNS:

In 1945 there was a fan contest to decide what the name of this Cleveland team would be, and the fans chose Browns after Ohio star and Bengals owner, Paul Brown.

DALLAS COWBOYS:

Representing the "Lone Star State," Texas, the Dallas Cowboys made sure to include the now-famous blue and white star on their uniforms.

DENVER BRONCOS:

During a contest in 1960, fans chose the name Broncos, which are known as wild and rough horses and pictured as such in the team's uniform.

DETROIT LIONS:

After failing to make money, a radio station bought the Detroit Spartans and made them the Detriot Lions, named after the baseball team Detroit Tigers. More than anything, the owner wanted the team to be the ruler of the NFL, like the lion is the ruler of the jungle.

GREEN BAY PACKERS:

Taking the name Packers from the Indian Packing Company, which helped buy the team's first uniforms, the Green Bay Packers used a football-shaped G to represent Green Bay.

HOUSTON TEXANS:

The Houston NFL searched long for a name and came up with the Bobcats, Stallions, Texans, Toros, and Apollos. So, after putting out an online survey, the public chose the Texans. To represent the state, owner Bob McNair chose a bull's head split open, to look like the Texas flag.

INDIANAPOLIS COLTS:

Originally the Baltimore Colts, their name comes from Charles Evans, who won the name-the-team contest. Since Baltimore was known for horse racing, it fit perfectly to have that name and a horseshoe on the uniforms.

JACKSONVILLE JAGUARS:

The logo of the Jacksonville Jaguars was met with uncertainty. The owners of the Jaguar car, Ford Motor Company, said the logos looked too similar, and did not want the team using it. After talking, however, they worked together and named the Jaguar the official car of the Jaguars.

KANSAS CITY CHIEFS:

After moving to Kansas City, owner Lamar Hunt and coach Hank Stram wanted to keep the name Texans, but after a fan contest decided the name Chiefs, he agreed. The new name would honor Mayor Bartle, whose nickname was Chief while working for the Boy Scouts of America.

MIAMI DOLPHINS:

In 1965 the name Miami Dolphins was chosen to be the new Florida team in a contest, by over 600 people. The owner Joe Robbie was proud of this logo since the dolphin was known to be smart and fast; exactly what a football team needs.

MINNESOTA VIKINGS:

Bert Rose wanted a team that was built to be strong and to win. So, he recommended the name Vikings since it represented aggression and the will to win, along with the Nordic traditions of the Northern Midwest.

NEW ENGLAND PATRIOTS:

Patriots, who were rebels during the American Revolution, were chosen to represent New England. This was a popular pick by the voters when a contest was introduced to choose the name.

NEW ORLEANS SAINTS:

With a large population who celebrate All Saints Day, the name Saints was perfect for this New Orleans team. The team also followed the state flag by using the fleur-de-lis, lily in French, on their uniform.

NEW YORK GIANTS:

Like other early NFL teams, the New York Giants took the same name as one of their baseball teams, but, gave themselves an All-American look with red, white, and blue decorating their uniforms.

NEW YORK JETS:

In 1963 the New York Titans were changed to the New York Jets. This was thought to be just right since their new stadium would be between LaGuardia and Kennedy airports, and the United States thought it was entering the "jet" age, when man would live on the moon.

OAKLAND RAIDERS:

In 1960, after a contest by the *Oakland Tribune* left the city with the name Oakland Señors, so many people made fun of the name that the owners decided to change it. So, nine days later, they agreed on the Oakland Raiders, which came in third place in the contest.

PHILADELPHIA EAGLES:

This NFL team got its name and logo from the Blue Eagle, which was used to show progress and better days during The Great Depression.

PITTSBURGH STEELERS:

Pittsburgh's logo actually came from the "Steelmark" by Pittsburgh U.S. Steel, who asked the team to wear the logo on their helmets for one game. After winning this game, the team wanted to keep it, so they still wear it today.

SAN DIEGO CHARGERS:

In a name-the-team contest in 1960, Gerald Courtney submitted the Chargers as the team's name, and won. The Chargers' logo then used a bolt of lightning to show the electricity the team will build during games.

SAN FRANCISCO 49ERS:

Named after the people who rushed to the west in search of gold, the San Francisco 49ers wore red and gold to bring the gold rush to the football field.

SEATTLE SEAHAWKS:

In 1975 a contest proved that many people in Seattle wanted their team to be named after the powerful Seahawk.

ST. LOUIS RAMS:

Can you believe that the name Rams actually has nothing to do with St. Louis? General manager Damon Wetzel's favorite football team was the Fordham Rams, so he took it to St. Louis. As for the horns, a college student drew up the original horns because he thought it would look good on the helmet.

TAMPA BAY BUCCANEERS:

What's better than a logo made from a legend? The Tampa Bay Buccaneers, who got their name through a name-the-team contest, was chosen because of the Southwest Florida legend of Pirates. They have named their own pirate Captain Fear, and he is there to take down the competition.

TENNESSEE TITANS:

While they used to be the Tennessee Oilers, this team changed their name in 1999 to represent their strength and skills. They also put a flame on their uniform to show off their power in the game of football.

WASHINGTON REDSKINS:

The team originated in Boston and was named the Boston Braves baseball team. It was renamed the Redskins in 1932 and the name was retained when the team moved to Washington in 1937.

ABOUT THE AUTHORS

TIKI BARBER grew up in Roanoke, Virginia, where he wore number 2 for the Cave Spring Eagles during junior high school. From 1997 through 2006 he wore number 21 as running back for the New York Giants, where he holds every rushing record in team history. He lives in New York.

RONDE BARBER wore number 5 for the Cave Spring Eagles. Today he is one of the top cornerbacks in the NFL and wears number 20 for the Tampa Bay Buccaneers. Ronde is a Super Bowl champion, a five-time Pro Bowl selection, and the first cornerback in the history of the league to have at least twenty-five sacks and forty interceptions in a career. He lives in Florida with his wife, Claudia, and their daughters.

TIKI AND RONDE BARBER have collaborated on eight other children's books, *By My Brother's Side,* the Christopher Award–winning *Game Day*, *Teammates*, *Kickoff!*, *Go Long!*, *Wild Card*, *Red Zone*, and most recently *Goal Line.*

PAUL MANTELL is the author of many books for young readers, including books in the Hardy Boys and Matt Christopher series.